Vèvè-Punk: Birth of the Dream

Dominick Rabrun

Blue Cerberus

Illustrations by Dominick Rabrun

Cover Design by Damon Freeman

ISBN: 978-1-944744-40-3

First Edition : January 2026

Contents

For my mother, Guylene Rabrun, who taught me to love knowledge

INTRODUCTION

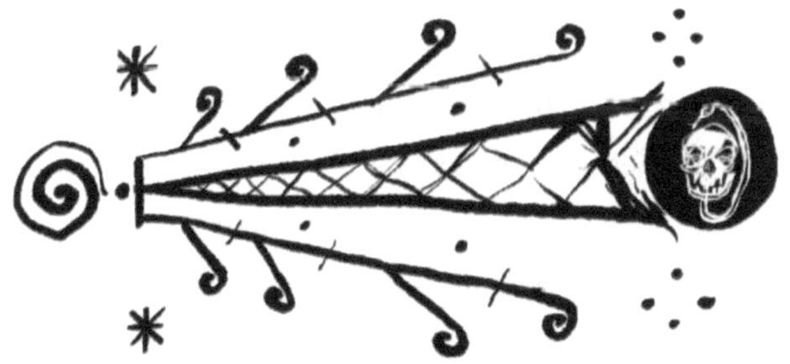

Growing up, Vodou was a dirty word in my household. Any attempts I made to ask about it were cut off with rejection, rebukes, or redirection towards Jehovah. I was told many times by my aunt that in our family "We don't do that," and that it was simply a Satanic thing that people did back home in Haiti. End of story.

But there were always mysteries and contradictions. I can name a handful of times when someone in my family fell ill, and there were whispers of someone having caused it from afar through some ritual. The title "Bondye" was always the Most High at home, and I knew it was different from what Jehovah's Witnesses wanted it to mean for us. It was also somehow synonymous with Jehovah or God.

If your knowledge of Vodou, or "Voodoo," was anything like mine, your understanding of the religion is limited to depictions of black people stabbing dolls with pins or dancing in ceremonies of dubious origin.

After I left the Jehovah's Witnesses at 19, I began a long, slow process of educating myself on Haitian history. I learned about Toussaint Louverture, the Haitian Revolution, and the consequences of freedom that are still embedded in how Haiti and its people have existed since the 18th century. My journey to educate myself on the history of my ancestors brought me to learning about Vodou, or "Vodoun."

This is my definition: Vodou is a mixture of spiritualities and ideologies brought by our West African ancestors to places like Haiti, Jamaica, Cuba, and Brazil. In addition, the practices of Obeah, Candomblé, and Santería, etc. were inspired by this diaspora.

I am not an expert on Vodou, but I would argue that no one is—and that's the point. If you ask two practitioners what Vodou is, you'll get two beautiful, contradictory, and mysterious answers. Vodou is a mystery, and it's as mysterious as the fact that I can use these symbols we call "letters" and "words" to transmit my thoughts into your mind right now.

The more I learn about Haitian history and Vodou, the more questions I have. My journey has provided me with answers in the form of a mythology that started revealing itself to me sometime right before COVID broke out in 2020. *Vèvè-Punk* is my attempt at answering a lot of questions that don't have clean answers in this life:

- Why did my parents die of HIV-related illnesses in the early '90s while living in the wealthiest nation on Earth?

- If there is a difference between Bondye and Jehovah, who would win in a fight?

- What if Loas—Vodou spirits—became corporations in 2002 and rendered our capitalist economic system useless?

- What if Haitian descendants became the most powerful and influential beings on the planet?

Vèvè-Punk is my creative world where tradition and innovation coexist, fusing together *vèvès,* ancient Haitian Vodou symbols, with modern technology. This collection critiques how corporations, like modern *Loas,* consume our energy, turning us into fuel for their growth. *Vèvè-Punk* reclaims this energy, channeling it into resistance and empowerment.

At its core, *Vèvè-Punk* celebrates the resilience of Haitian heritage. Vèvès and cosmograms are treated as gateways to infinite complexity, challenging us to see beyond the surface and into the vast potential of every symbol. This philosophy is a conversation about liberation, identity, and the power of cultural legacy in a digital age.

I've included a glossary and a recommended reading list at the end of this book to explain some terms and concepts. If you find yourself scratching your head and looking for clear, canonical answers, though, I hate to burst your bubble—but it ain't happening. Welcome to *Vèvè-Punk*.

Ednice and the Gardener

Ednice stomped on bright, pungent flowers on her way to convince the hermit in the pink house to sign a paper. Humid mountain air caused strange foliage to bloom in L'Après, the land of the dead. Too many shades of shiny orange, pink, blue, and creamy white flowers of all sorts of sizes and shapes grazed Ednice's ankles, tugged at her dress and her travel bag. She knew the smelliest flowers to avoid, this being her fourth time travelling into this remote mountain valley. If her life—or, well, afterlife—were a story, this would be the part where something powerful and true would happen. *And then, the lowly Visitor relegated to being an unpaid bill collector felt a sign that came from the wind!*

For a moment there, Ednice almost believed her own story, as it coiled around her mind the way any good story always did. The pink house was there in the distance now, surrounded by more waist-high flowers and izipeñas—pesky hummingbirds. There was no wind, though, and certainly no sign that anything was going to be different. Her stories never came true, and they stayed locked away inside of her, for that was the will of Jehovah and the Beholders!

"But wait!" Ednice pronounced at the fragrant flowers that bent under her persistent march. There was a possibility that her story *would* change this time. Because *this* time, the crochety, elusive hermit would open the door and sign the paper, and... The rest of the story unraveled in her mind, clear as the blue and pink pastel sky.

She would be Speaker Regis, not Visitor Regis.

As Speaker Regis, she might be able to weave bits of truth into her stories. Not the lies and propaganda she had been telling for years just to survive in this place. There had to be others like her out there who secretly dreamed of a L'Après free from the ever-present eye of Jehovah and the Beholders. If she did not become a Speaker, her will to survive would wither away eventually. She would make some mistake and say the wrong thing, and a group of her peers would erase her from reality like she never existed at all. The higher she could climb in Beholder rank, the safer she might be from being vanished.

"...And that's what happened." Ednice called the end of the tale to a group of izipeñas that buzzed in front of the pink house.

"Isn't that a good story?"

The izipeñas had no response to this. Ednice sucked her teeth and pulled a small jar of honeywater from her bag. "You all don't deserve a good story. You don't give me any feedback, or constructive criticism." She knelt among the reeking flowers and unscrewed the jar, leaving it out for them to drink. The izipeñas, which usually buzzed too close to her head and made her yelp, kept their distance for now as she looked up at the house.

It was more like a two-floor shack of chipped pink wood planks all nailed together. *The hermit was likely not a craftsman,* she thought as she adjusted her dress and climbed those three creaky front porch steps. The roof was mostly made of hammered tin, just like the houses of the farmers in Haiti. But there was no Haiti here, no Earth or Pan-Caribbean African Union like when she had been alive. There was only L'Après, and this ugly shack of a house.

Ednice raised her fist and knocked, for what she hoped would be the last time.

"Hello?" she called and knocked again. No answer. She tried the formal call that she knew by heart. "This is Visitor Regis from the Beholders, and I am here to ask you to sign your oath to serve the will of Jehovah! Your safety in this paradise isn't guaranteed otherwise." No answer. Ednice peeked through the windows, but they were so dark that they only showed her reflection. She looked as scared as she felt, the whites of her dry eyes large against her dark skin.

Perhaps this was some kind of test, Ednice considered as she turned to face the porch and look out at the izipeñas sipping at her drink. But if this was a test, she did not know who it had come from. It could not be Jehovah. She had stopped praying to Him years back, when she accepted that if He did speak or respond to anyone, it had never been her. The thought was freeing, dangerous. A secret she kept coiled in her brain, just like her stories.

One of these stories sprang forth and scratched her mind—this one a barbed and ugly flower. She imagined Speaker Arnaud's response when she came back with the final declaration on the paper that would read, "RESURRECTED MOUNTAIN HERMIT DID NOT ANSWER." That written declaration would bar Ednice from any chance of a promotion beyond Visitor forever. Her only option would be to continue knocking on doors to get confused people to sign their afterlives away to an ideology that she didn't believe in.

Ednice clenched her jaw and turned back around, shredding the barbed, ugly story in her mind. If this was her last moment as a potential storyteller in this beautiful, boring, pastel, terrifying prison of an eternal world, she would live it by telling a true story.

She turned, faced the door, took a big gulp of air, and called out like the storytellers of her childhood in Haiti once did.

"Krik?" A melodic, plaintive sound, begging—enticing. She aimed it at the door, at the house, at L'Après and the hermit inside and the izipeñas and anyone who would listen.

No answer, but a breeze that rustled her dress and her hat, carrying less of the flower smell and something else—but she didn't know what, because a story was coming out of her now, from her toes and through her stomach and loud from her mouth.

"Maybe you don't understand, but I'll explain to you. I am a storyteller, and in this ancient form of creation, we call out that word that was first uttered by Bondye, the One We Cannot See, when the universe was created. I am going to ask Krik again, and when I say Krik, you are going to respond with Krak! if you want to hear a story. And if you don't, I'm going to tell you it anyway, because I am going to have to walk back home and give up all my dreams. So, I'm going to say it one more time. Krik?"

Ednice took in air, balling up her fists. At first, there was nothing. And then, a low, slow rumble that rocked the foundation of the house and made her cry out in excitement.

"Krak?" the mumble responded.

Ednice licked her lips, suddenly aware of her thirst and how quiet everything was now. There was nothing but her and the story and the door in front of her. It trembled, creaking open a fraction as she continued.

"Once upon a time, there was a Beholder living in the afterlife named Visitor Regis, and every day she knocked on the door of a mysterious hermit because she wanted him to sign a paper pledging allegiance to Jehovah—"

At the sound of that name, the door started to close. Ednice hissed and shoved her foot in the gap, but it was like pushing against a wall of concrete.

"—At least let me in so I can tell you the rest of the story!" The door paused, then began to open again, inch by inch. Ednice kept her foot on the threshold as it revealed a large man standing in the doorway, almost filling it. When he spoke, it was a resonant rumble that Ednice could feel in her skin, vibrating from her fingertips to her chest as she stood there, looking like she was ready to force her way into the house.

"Now I'm curious," he said, with slow gaps between words. "What happens next?"

It was the hermit. The hermit was real, and he had answered, and he was most definitely a man, at least one head taller than her.

Ednice opened her mouth, then shut it as her words fled. She could not believe her fortune, or was it the result of her boldness? She strained to focus on the man's facial expression, but he was indistinct, difficult to pin any detail to. Not memorable at all, besides the complexion of his skin. Blue-black, like hers. And some kind of forgettable peasant cloth shirt that hid powerful, lean muscles, and big, calloused hands that gripped the doorframe. Those *hands*. Ednice stared at them, and—

"Hello?" the man boomed at her, through her.

Ednice blinked away the momentary stupor, pulling her determined foot back to her side of the threshold. "Thank you for opening your door to me." She bowed her head lower than was customary. On raising her gaze to meet his, she found the hermit appeared to be larger somehow, but not imposing. *Glowing* was the word that came to her.

"I would be happy to finish that story—I have many, but I would like for you to sign this paper first." To demonstrate, she plucked it from her travel bag along with a black ink pen.

The man said nothing, looking deflated in the shoulders, sagging out of...what? Disappointment?

"I'm Visitor Regis," she repeated. "May I ask your name?"

The man seemed to ponder this as he rocked from side to side, and he released his grip on the doorframe. "I just go by the Gardener these days," he said, the boom back in his voice and back in Ednice's body.

"It's a pleasure to meet you, Gardener." It was a strange name, but what wasn't strange in L'Après? She could not remember the last time she had been so nervous, so excited like this. A hard wind blew and yanked the paper out of her hand and to his feet, between them. The man stepped back into his house instead of reaching for it. Ednice apologized as she bent down to get it, stashing it back in her bag.

"No, I should have invited you in," the Gardener said, standing a foot or two in his house now. "I apologize." He looked smaller, wringing his hands. "Visitor Regis, would you like to come in? You've traveled far. I have water. I can cook you something and you can tell me the rest of that delightful story."

Ednice forced a smile and looked past the man into his pink house. She could spot nothing of interest, no sign that he was going to do anything but listen to her and then sign the paper. The improvised story from before still sat in her throat, eager to find an audience. And here was someone willing to listen. That was worth riding the strangeness, the power of this moment.

"I'd love to," she blurted out and stepped past the threshold in one motion, pushing through her better judgment and into the Gardener's home.

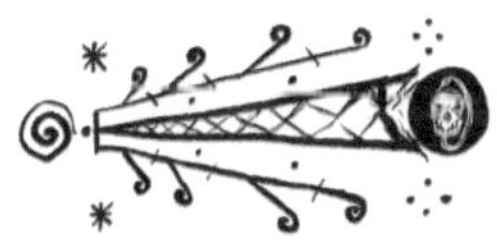

The pale pink house smelled of warm butter, caramel, and herbs. It looked larger on the inside than it was on the outside, made mostly of wood and some concrete. The tin ceiling was higher than it should have been, and she could not touch it by raising her hand. The Gardener approached without a sound, handing her a cup of creamy coffee—not water as he had promised earlier.

"Thank you," she said, and the man again seemed to fill up from these words. He stood taller, smiled in a boyish, proud way that made her giggle then look somewhere else.

"Is the coffee all right?" he asked.

"It's more than all right. It's *perfect,*" she said. "This is exactly how I used to like my coffee. Before..." She shrugged, sitting in a wicker chair he offered to her.

"Before you died and were resurrected to L'Après?" The Gardener sat in his own wicker chair in front of her. "I would love to know the story of L'Après, as you see it. Pretend like I don't know anything." His eager voice resonated through her again, through the chair beneath her.

"I could try," she said. It would be a unique challenge. She gestured with her coffee cup as she spoke, taking care to make this *her* version of the truth. But first, she filled her lungs with air and asked, "Krik?" Did the Gardener want to hear the story?

"Krak," responded the Gardener with a deep, resonating eagerness. He *did* want to hear the story. Ednice started:

"In the beginning, Bondye and Jehovah were two hungry twin brothers who loved to bake. Bondye was the powerful older brother but wasn't ambitious. Jehovah was the younger ambitious brother, but he coveted Bondye's power. They baked cookies one at a time, and they were the strangest cookies—made from time and space and emotion.

"One day, they created their greatest cookie that Bondye designed. It had everything in it, good and bad. Bondye thought all the elements should be kept together and they could start on the next cookie. Jehovah seethed, disagreeing. He wanted to break it up into pieces and then take them all for himself. He was done working with his brother. In fact, he wanted to design all the cookies and baked goods from then on."

The Gardener sat forward on the edge of his chair, unblinking. Ednice felt his attention on her like a warm sunbeam, urging her to continue.

"They fought over the cookie, and it broke into three parts. Those parts grew and grew as the brothers shouted at each other. Meanwhile, the three pieces floated above and below them, growing larger. They had to do something to stop it. Bondye had a plan as usual, but Jehovah didn't like it. So, they split, trying to control the three cookie pieces.

"Those cookie pieces are now stacked on one another and became the three worlds we know of. At the top, there's the world we can't see—a big, ethereal cookie where Bondye and Jehovah live on opposite sides because they're still mad at each other. Then there's L'Avant, a solid, crunchy cookie, which is what we call the land of the living. That's where we're born for the first time, I suppose. And die. And then there's L'Après at the bottom, a kind of in-between, mushy cookie. That's the land of the dead, where we are now. And it's where we're going to stay."

Ednice let out a long breath and eased back in her chair, allowing a moment of silence to punctuate the story's end.

"I *like* that story." The Gardener smiled, drumming his hands on his lap in a nameless, upbeat rhythm. "I like how you explain big things and make them real. And you know how to hide some truth inside of your stories."

The compliment was too much. Ednice mumbled a *thank you*, and the house seemed to shake as she put her coffee down and hunted for the paper. She needed to get back on track. She needed to...

"Can I make a suggestion?" the Gardener asked, but he went on before she could answer. "You're my guest, but can I please ask you to not use *that name* or talk about the Beholders while you're in my house?"

Ednice furrowed her brow. "What name? Jeho—"

"Yes, *that* name. Don't say it. And all of that, just..." With his large hand, the Gardener indicated her Beholder-issued scarf and straw hat that declared her rank. Ednice surprised herself by laughing, and he laughed too. He continued, sipping at his own coffee. "I want to know about *you*. I want more stories!"

Ednice noticed the way he leaned forward with his coffee cup, and she could see his eyes now. How vast and dark they were. Hungry eyes, the eyes of a student who was eager to give and take of her memories and knowledge and stories. Perhaps the Gardener contained stories that were worth telling. How could she resist?

During her next sip, she calculated. She could tell Speaker Arnaud that the Resurrected nonbeliever was eager to learn—that was not a lie. A few more visits would be required to determine if the Gardener would indeed sign. She folded these treacherous thoughts away into the salted caramel and balanced cream in the coffee. Felt them dissolve with her momentary worry. They would bob back up later, but for now...

"I shouldn't be talking about myself, really..." But the coffee and the cushioned chair under her said that it was safe to do so in the warm house. So, Ednice took off her straw hat and her scarf, and she spoke slowly at first. "I've been in L'Après for about forty-eight years now. Haven't aged a day since I got here." She looked down at her hands holding the almost-empty coffee cup, feeling some embarrassment at this abomination of a body that was eternally in its late twenties.

The Gardener tilted his head, still leaning forward. "You don't like it here." A statement, not a question.

Ednice shook her head. Nodded. "No. I mean." This wasn't going well, but when was she ever honest? Who would this hermit tell, anyway?

"I hate it here sometimes. Most of the time," he said. "Over the years, only Beholders come up here to knock, and I usually don't answer, but you're different."

"Different how?" Ednice asked. The Gardener got out of the chair, went into his kitchen, and returned with a tray of butter cookies in stacks of three. She took a stack and examined it. One soft, one hard, and then an in-between cookie. When had he baked these, and why hadn't she smelled them until now? Ednice took a bite, tasting sweet almond and raspberry.

"You told me a story, and it wasn't what you've been told to say." The Gardener stood beside her, clearly checking to see how she liked the cookies.

"Oh. These are great, thank you."

The Gardener sat back down, looking pleased with himself.

Ednice crunched into the cookie, taking another bite. "But I'm not different, really. I'm just a Visitor sent to get you to sign a document. Well, a very eager Visitor who overstepped a bit."

Together, Ednice and the Gardener talked, and he kept her coffee cup full. Mostly he asked her questions and requested that she answer in small stories. He was thoughtful and greedy with his inquiries into her. Delighted when she acknowledged that he had got something right or could predict how something would go. When the sun started to set, he insisted on cooking her a dinner of roast chicken and mais moulen. How could he know her favorite dish?

"I have to get going back down the mountain to catch a carriage. It'll be dark soon." Ednice collected her straw hat and scarf, making her way out the door before he could protest. She secretly wanted him to protest, though she did not intend on staying.

"Will you come by for dinner soon? Tomorrow, maybe?" The Gardener stood on the threshold, and Ednice was already down the front porch steps when she turned around to see him in his doorway. *He doesn't come out of there.* It was a casual thought, but one that would stick around and grow in its stubbornness.

"I'll try," she said, already practicing her excuse for why she would need an extension for the signing.

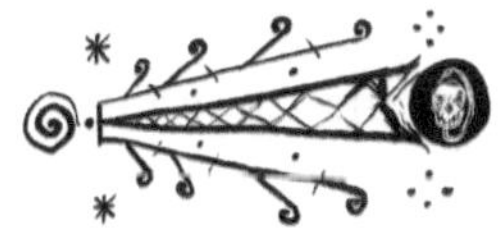

The Gardener's pink house on the mountain grew brighter each time Ednice returned. The flowers seemed healthier, their fragrance mild and alluring. Even the izipeñas buzzed more carefully on her return. How could she have been annoyed at these beautiful creatures in this place of raw truth and freedom? One bold orange and purple izipeña zoomed up to greet Ednice, tongue darting in and out and chirping what sounded like "krik krik?"

"You've got half of it right, at least." Ednice laughed and left a new jar of honeywater on the porch step. She took off her straw hat and scarf. Checked in the window to make sure her hair was in place, straightened the neck of her blouse. The door opened without her knocking, and the Gardener stood there ready to rumble a greeting of *Krik?* To which she would answer with enthusiasm, *Krak!*

It was a game. Who would say it first? She went inside and they had coffee and warm snacks in their respective chairs. It felt wrong sometimes, like a betrayal, but there was also possibility here. The Gardener's house felt like the only real place in L'Après, where Ednice could say anything if it was true. Which is what she began to do.

"I feel like everything in L'Après is a lie," Ednice whispered. The Gardener pressed his lips together into a hard line and made a concerned sound. *Hmmph.*

"It is a pretty prison, isn't it?" He stood from his chair and looked out of his porch window. *It's true,* Ednice thought. She really could tell him anything in this house, and he wouldn't shun her, or report her. Seeing his broad back gave Ednice extra courage.

She got up and went to see what he saw. The curious orange and purple izipeña was on the windowsill, flicking out its tongue and looking back at them. Ednice spoke to that izipeña through the window, though the words were meant for the Gardener. "Everyone pretends in L'Après just to survive. I'm pretending too, most of the time. And I get so *lonely* here even though I have so many people around me."

This was dangerous—it was too true. Speaker Arnaud had lectured Ednice about not getting the signing, and she allowed a few more visits, but soon she would simply deem Ednice's efforts as failed.

"Are you lonely when you're with me?" the Gardener asked, turning to face her.

"No." The answer came too quick for her to stop it, and she shook with a small fright.

"I feel the same." The floorboards beneath her and her heart quaked in time with the Gardener's footsteps towards her. He held out one of his big hands and she stepped back, but *why* was she reaching out to grasp it, and *why* was she letting him pull her up into his arms and oh *god* he smelled just like every perfect dinner and cup of coffee all at once.

She murmured in gasps. It was hard to breathe against his solid chest and shoulders. "I don't even know your name. This is stupid. Just...could you just sign the paper and I'll go away. People are going to ask questions, and then they'll come to find you."

The Gardener stopped Ednice with a look. As close as she had ever dared to look into his eyes, which were black and as bright and vast as the night sky, and her heart was hammering in her ears, and something inside her was unraveling.

They kissed, and the house sighed around them, glowing a warm orange. Ednice blinked and tried to inspect that glow but instead kissed him again. And again.

The Gardener took her by the hand and led her through the house and into his bedroom, which only held a bed large enough for him, but it was clean and they could use it just fine. Ednice kicked off her clothes, and his hands were exploring her as if she were a precious sculpture. She folded down to her knees, crying with the sudden realization of it all, and he was down there with her, holding her and saying nothing, asking nothing.

When she thanked him for that—for the nothing—he brightened and wrote messages on her skin with the tips of his fingers. The messages were funny, soft tickling things, until they grew firm and eager. Ednice wanted him then, and he asked if she was sure. She was.

Ednice drew in the feelings of guilt and shame and let them burn inside of her. The Gardener was a capable lover, though he was as out of practice as she was. The story they told with their bodies and breathing was ancient, wordless. When she praised the man's effort, it made him grow and fill her more. But there was a vulnerability when he waned or let her take control in her way. A temporariness that seemed to make him nervous. After, as she began to get dressed, she asked him about this phenomenon, seeking some kind of way to make sense of what had just happened.

"Do you feel like you're worthy without me having to tell you?"

The Gardener thought about this, and by the time he answered, she had her clothes on. "I don't know," he said. "But it feels right when you say it."

Ednice touched his graying hair, his stubbled jaw. "Stay here tonight," he said, wrapping his arms around her waist. And then, as an afterthought, "Please."

She shouldn't. She needed his signature soon, and she'd already missed the last carriage home. She would have to make the whole trip by foot. "I can't," she said, and the Gardener released her. She picked up her bag and produced the paper and black ink pen. "Just sign, and I'll figure out a way to get back here, or make sure no one finds you—"

It wasn't a shout, but the Gardener's voice was so loud it made her ears hurt. "I don't need your help to hide." He looked down at the paper. "Is your rank in that foolish cult all you care about?" His words were spikes coated in venom. Ednice took two big steps back, the shock still registering in her body.

The Gardener tensed and drew up, a coiled rattlesnake ready to sting. His big hands curled into fists on muscled thighs. Panting, though not from the efforts of love. The house was suddenly cold enough to see her breath fogging up in front of her face. Ednice smelled the antiseptic of the hospital from when she had been alive but dying, heard the beeping of an EKG. It was so real that she turned, looked up and around, expecting to see the hospital bed she died in. Sobs and sniffles around her, coming from the ghosts of her family. The sickly-sweet smell of her death filling her nose.

"What are you doing?" She took her bag and stumbled out of the Gardener's bedroom, suppressing a gag. The hallway looked just like her apartment back in Dessalines where she had spent her greatest and worst times, and it bent and lurched, pitching her forward so that she was staggering and bouncing off the walls and screaming for help.

The Gardener's powerful grip took her by the shoulders, but Ednice hurled herself out the front door, still holding onto the unsigned paper. She wrenched herself from his grip and ran through his thorny garden as he called her name in giant bellows that made the flowers shrivel and droop away.

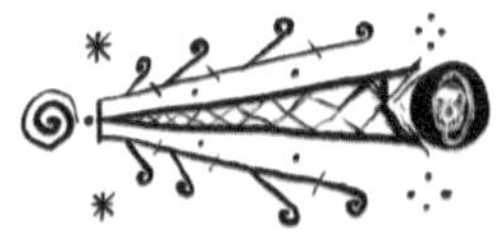

Sour, rotten sulfur. That's what the roses in the garden smelled like as Ednice hurried towards the Gardener's house, which was the color of dried pink vomit. The flowers gave little dying gasps as she went, looking down at the paper in her hand. She didn't need to read it to know what was on there; it was on repeat in her mind:

Visitor Regis, I regret to inform you that you will never attain the rank of Speaker. However, you may bask in the knowledge that Jehovah made this decision, and not I.

—Speaker Arnaud

Ednice stomped up the steps and clenched her fists to hammer on the stupid small door. Then she kicked it, shouting, "Come out! Come out and see what you did, 'Gardener,' if that's your real name!"

The door swung open, and Ednice looked away as she held the paper in front of his face. He took her wrist when it was past the threshold and gently lowered it along with the paper. "Hello, Visitor Regis. I'm sorry about before."

Ednice swallowed a hard lump rising in her throat. "Look at what it says." She pulled away from him and held the paper up, on the other side of the door, where she knew he would not touch or follow her. "You *can* read, right?"

The Gardener held onto the door jamb, knuckles trembling. Ednice tensed up to protect herself against his tricks; she had grieved before and she would grieve again, but she would not be made into a fool.

"It wasn't supposed to be like this," he said.

Ednice shook the paper. "No more riddles. I'm never going to be a Speaker, and it's because of you and your stupid house and because you... you *did things* to my head, and I trusted you." She lowered the paper and held it against her thigh, where he had touched and caressed her only a few nights before. "And I was going to just burn this paper and never come back, but then I thought that I should come here one last time and tell you a story about yourself for a change, since you like to get your ego stroked so much. Krik?"

"Don't." The Gardener got that impossibly dark look in his eyes again. The lights behind him in his house dimmed, and the sound of thunder shook the porch, flattening the moment, sucking the air from Ednice's lungs, but she croaked on through it, standing as tall as she dared.

"You were never going to sign the paper, because you're a heretic, and you're the worst kind of Resurrected. I should *report* you. How about that?" Ednice panted, feeling lightheaded. Twinkling lights swayed in her vision, and her stomach churned.

"Can I speak now?" The Gardener stepped back, now holding a coffee pot. "Come in and just listen to my story. And if you hate it, you can leave forever. But I would dislike that."

She should leave right now. This was probably part of some torment that Jehovah had set for her. But one last conversation wouldn't hurt. Just one last sip of that damn perfect coffee.

"No," she said. "You can speak, but I'm not going in there with you."

The Gardener let go of the coffee pot, and instead of crashing to the floor it hung in the air for a moment, then dissolved like vapor. Ednice shrugged, pretending not to be impressed by the magic trick. She continued to look at him as the inside of his house glowed that hot orange, lighting him from behind. When he spoke next, his voice boomed from the house itself, though he didn't move his lips.

"I won't sign that paper because I refuse to worship a lost, greedy shard of Myself."

Ednice turned away from the brightness, more irritated than impressed now. "Come on, now you're just lying again. That's what you do: lie and take my time. Just be honest!" She laughed at the ridiculousness of this man trying to look so large and important to her, even though it was partially working. It was still a lie. "You didn't even do krik-krak. You're an awful storyteller."

The orange lights dimmed, and the Gardener spoke with his mouth, looking confused at her laughter. "I am not joking. I'm finally telling you the truth. I am Bondye."

Ednice laughed so hard that she almost fell onto her backside. She had to hold onto the porch railing to keep from dropping. "Hold... hold on..." She wheezed. "You're telling me that *you're* Bon-Bondyeeeee?"

"Yes."

"Bondye, the name of the... great creator that we used back in Haiti?"

"Yes."

Now she had the power and closure she needed to leave this strange man. She gathered herself, and her laughter turned into icy daggers she knew would stab him. "You know, I thought you were insane before, but now you're *really* showing yourself. Goodbye. And I know you're trapped in your house, so enjoy your loneliness. I... I thought you were different."

Stupid. Why did she even admit that? Stupid! Ednice went down the steps and into the field of flowers, which were now all fully withered and gray-brown. *I ignore those,* she thought, just keep on walking. She intended to, had been set to march out of this miserable place, but slowed down when the mountain path and flowers in the distance all lost their color. The withered flowers crunched under her and dissolved, just like the coffee pot had.

She whirled around to see the Gardener standing on the porch of his house, which was shivering and threatening to break down. The man—or the being who she had thought was the Gardener—shook on his feet, emaciated and colorless as he looked at her through those intense eyes. He took one step down from the porch toward the garden and missed. His leg folded and dissolved from under him, and his mouth stretched into a cavernous grimace. It took forever and no time for the rest of him to sit down, still clutching onto the rail.

The impact shook the field with a great quake that threw Ednice forward and onto the dirt that now had no smell. From the ground, she could see the buzzing izipeñas dropping from the air, plopping down around her with muted thumps. "No, please—" Ednice scrambled to gather as many of the small birds as she could, taking extra care with the orange and purple izipeña from before.

"What are you *doing?*" Ednice shouted at the Gardener, but the sound thinned and bent toward the cavernous, rippling grimace where his mouth should be. She got up, careful not to crush the birds in her arms while running to the porch.

"Don't... go..." The Gardener held her arm as she helped the man onto his one good leg and pulled him into the doorway of the house, now a jagged triangle she feared might slice them both. But she knew that she could not leave him here, no matter what he was. If she left him and the izipeñas out here, she would not be able to forgive herself.

As Ednice helped him along the threshold, a part of her thought, *I just need him to make those cups of coffee.* All of this, her life or afterlife, was so ridiculous that she collapsed in front of his wicker chair and laughed as she let the izipeñas buzz free.

There was color in the world again. Warmth and stability. No more thunderclaps and withering dead objects. Ednice breathed in hard gasps, watching the izipeñas flit around the house. Warm hands helped Ednice up to a seated position on the floor. The Gardener sat beside her, holding a coffee and looking skinny and tired. But both his leg and his house had returned. The sky beyond the open door had returned to its original color. Ednice took the cup and sipped.

"Can you... forgive me?" The Gardener exhaled the words, and Ednice felt the purity of them in her mind, as strong and sweet as the taste of the drink.

"Be quiet," she replied, though it was with a softness. "What *was* that?"

"I told you," he said. "I am Bondye."

"Hold on, I'm not ready to say your name yet."

"Okay," the Gardener (Bondye?) said.

Ednice sipped again, leaning back against His wicker chair.

"So, You're the creator of... everything."

"Yes. Well. I'm more like a concentrated aspect of Myself, so that you can see and touch and talk to Me."

Ednice found it hard to look at Him now, but she tried to start by looking at His hands, which were becoming normal. "Did we almost die?"

"I would have died if you had not helped me back. *He* would have found me. You would have been safe, eventually."

"You don't sound so sure."

The Gardener smiled like He used to when she told Him a particularly mysterious story.

Ednice was not yet finished. Questions came to her in waves, in between moments where she was astounded that she was still talking to Him, or anyone. "So... I've been sleeping with God?"

Bondye stuck out His lower lip in a thoughtful expression, then did one of His *hmms,* as if it puzzled Him too.

"What do you mean, hmm? You're You!"

"I am. But I don't want this to change things. That's what I was afraid of."

Ednice got up, putting her coffee in the sink. "Why are you telling me this? Why now?"

The Gardener followed her, but at arm's length. "Because I've been watching you for a long time, and I am stuck here, and I need someone I can trust to help tell My story to the world. It's the only way I'll be able to escape."

She stiffened, her vision swimming. The walls felt like they were closing in on her. "You've been... watching me?" Why had He not said this before? Flashes of her life rushed through her mind. Had He been watching her since she was a child, calling out to Him and hearing silence? "How long?" she asked.

"I watched you when I could," He said, though that didn't offer any consolation. Ednice pulled away, wanting to run, but where would she go? How could she go now that she had this true story to tell?

"I am in love with you," the Gardener said.

Ednice kept her eyes on the porcelain sink and its many grooves. It was no wonder He loved it when she thanked or praised Him in any way. "How can You love me? You don't even... I haven't even told You my name, or anything about me, really—"

"You're really going to make me do this?" He asked. The house seemed to expand and took on the same shape of her childhood home. She could hear her grandmother shouting from somewhere. The Gardener spoke. "You're Ednice Regis. You were born in Cap-François in 1952. Your mother's name was Geraldine—"

"Stop."

"You loved to tell stories more than anything else. And now you're helping Me with your stories."

Ednice took her hand away and rubbed at her face. She felt the house bend again, and it smelled like coffee, like Him.

"I didn't mean to scare you. I've been lonely, and this is new for me."

Ednice nodded, faced Him with her body now, clutching her hands in front of her. "Can we start over?"

"Restarting time? That would be very difficult, and I can't do that while I'm trapped—"

"No, I mean us. We can start over again and tell stories, like before. And You can tell me everything, and I'll tell You everything, but You have to act like

You don't know already, like before. And I'm not calling You... well, Your name."

The Gardener rocked back and forth on His heels, grinning. "Yes. You will stay with me, then? And help me?"

"Slow down," Ednice said, shaking her head. "You can start with telling me where You keep the food here, if any of it is real. I can fix us something to eat."

The Gardener led her to an icebox, and together they prepared a meal in relative silence.

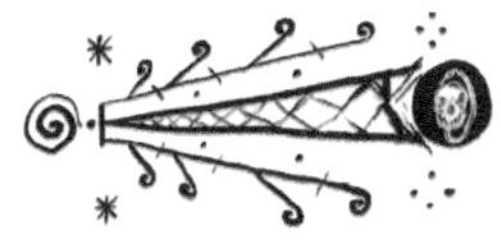

Later, after they had gone to bed and Ednice did her share of thanking and praising, the Gardener whispered "Krik?" to her as she lay beside Him, more comfortable and safer than she had ever been in L'Après. Her eyelids lowered as she responded with a "Krak," and the house darkened, melted away to the shapeless, nameless void she went to in dreams.

The Gardener continued for some time, telling Ednice what she could grasp.

He repeated Himself when she asked Him to.

He slowed down when she asked Him to.

He told her the story of how Jehovah had trapped Him in this garden that was not a garden, and why He could not leave yet.

He told her His plan to escape this place, and what He thought it might take.

"What do you need me to do?" Ednice whispered in the language of dreams.

"You will go back home with your paper, which I will sign with a story," Bondye said. "A story that will allow the Beholders and Jehovah to see what they want. You will become a Speaker."

Ednice nuzzled up to Him in the warm void but felt a slight fear. She would get what she initially wanted, but lose Him?

"No, I will send a part of Me with you," Bondye said, "in the form of izipeñas, My loyal birds. It is a form that no one will suspect. You will be able to use them to spread My stories and visit Me in dreams whenever you wish."

"Alright," Ednice agreed, feeling her cold, momentary fear melt away. In the corner of awareness, she saw the orange and purple izipeña from before, now full of honeywater and buzzing with a vibrant energy that sent waves of radiant warmth through her.

"You will spread the truth about Me and become My prophet," Bondye said.

"What?" This startled Ednice, even in dreams.

"Remember what I told you?" Bondye asked, holding her in a firm embrace. "That you can hide the truth inside of your stories?"

She did.

"I will help you to do that even more. You will help me gather strength and allies. And, most importantly, I will continue to love you as long as I am able."

Ednice returned the embrace with every bit of her mortal self, scared but trusting that this is why she was here in this land of resurrection and sadness. This is what she had been searching for. *He* was what she had been searching for.

"Merci, Bondye," Ednice said, and the Gardener filled with the orange glow that covered them both. In L'Après, nestled in the small house on the mountains surrounded by orange flowers, Ednice slept beside Bondye, whom she now loved, and in careful whispers, the two began to tell stories together. The orange and purple izipeña buzzed above their heads, eager to demonstrate its ability to imitate Ednice, the great storyteller.

"Krik?"

The Ongoing Revelation of Ednice Regis

KRIK?

KRAK!

This is everything I know, as told to me, Ednice
Regis, by Bondye, the One We Cannot See.

In the beginning, Bondye awoke from a long, dreamless sleep.

Using the gem of creation, Bondye made nothingness, somethingness, and everything in between.

He created the Earth, the animals, and the life that walks upon it. He formed the Loas—spirit-beings—and trained them with His hidden desires.

Not even the Loas could understand all Bondye's will.

Bondye said to the living things, "I am Bondye. Call Me what you like, as long as it is true."

He built a tropical island, cultivated a farm, and settled down in His house.

Before resting, He created a skeleton who was ridden by a figure coated in blood, saying, "I will call you Kenbe La. One day, you will be the greatest of the Loas. I will forget you now, lest I need you later."

Bondye laid down His gem of creation and went to sleep, forgetting about Kenbe La.

"Do not bother me," He told the Loas. "Do as I plan—or don't. It is still My will."

The Loas asked, "What shall we call Your will?"

"Call it Vodou," said Bondye.

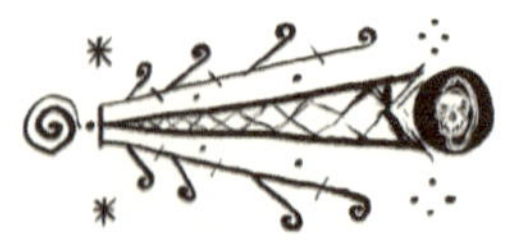

The Loas obeyed, and life evolved from tiny organisms to humans. These humans multiplied, were enslaved, fought, and survived.

Bondye dreamt while He slept and saw a great battle in the future. The dream showed Him suffering for Himself, the Loas, and humans.

When He woke, a large, white version of Himself sat by His bed. This figure wore a crown and held a scepter containing the gem of creation.

"Who are you?" asked Bondye with sleepy amusement. "And why do you have My gem?"

"I am Jehovah," said the other with a loud and shaky boastfulness. "I am the superior and true version of you. Now, you must enter the gem and surrender your power to Me."

Bondye laughed, saying, "*Gade moun sayo*! I am not an impostor; I am Myself."

Jehovah struck Bondye with the scepter, trapping Him inside the gem.

"How novel," thought Bondye. "A part of Me seeks to destroy Me. This will be the greatest story ever told."

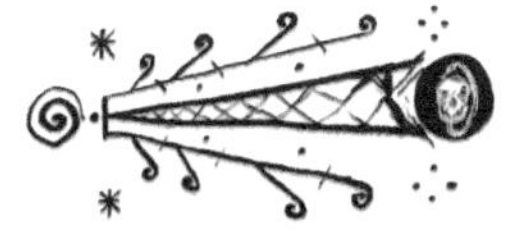

Jehovah sat on a golden throne and remade nothing-ness and somethingness in His vision. He created a new Earth, with angels and myths to serve Him.

Trapped in the gem, Bondye slept, woke, and sought a way to escape.

The Loas continued their tasks, battling humans and Jehovah's vengeful angels.

Yet I saw the ending, galloping through my memory and the future all at once.

When it seems all hope is lost, Kenbe La will usher in the Age of New Loas and will come to Bondye's aid.

BIRTH OF THE LOAS

In the beginning, Bondye—the One We Cannot See—moved through nothingness, shaping existence with His creation gem. With ultimate precision, He crafted galaxies, supernovae, and the tiniest quarks, all according to His design, which is sometimes called Vodou. And it was good enough.

But one day, Bondye encountered something peculiar: contradictions. There were things that resisted being created, slipping from His grasp and defying His gem's influence. These things refused to take form, existing and not existing all at once.

"How curious," Bondye said. He pursued them, calling out, but they evaded Him. This puzzled and hurt Bondye, and for the first time, He felt truly alone. There was no one to share His confusion, no one to help Him make sense of it.

In His solitude, Bondye resolved to create companions who could live in this space of contradiction, beings who would exist neither entirely in His realm nor the realm of the living. They would be companions, intermediaries, and reflections of His desires.

So, Bondye strained His energy and mind and, with great effort, birthed the Loas: spirit-beings who would exist between worlds. This space would be called *Lot Boa*.

The first to arrive was **Legba**, stepping forward at a pure moment of contradiction. "It is alright for contradictions to exist," Legba said with multiple voices. "These are also called paradoxes. I will remain in the spaces where choices are made. These spaces will be called crossroads. Or not."

Bondye agreed. "Welcome, Legba. You will start and end all communications between the Loas and Me."

Legba accepted this role, a quiet smile on his face as he stood at the threshold of possibility.

Next came the **Marassa Jumeaux**, who appeared as twin children but were also triplets. They laughed as they danced around Bondye and Legba.

"We're hungry," they said, their voices overlapping.

Bondye, surprised by their boldness, asked, "What will you eat?"

"Everything!" they replied, giggling as they snatched bits of light and darkness. "Feed us. House us. Dress us!"

Their insatiable hunger and mischievous demands made Bondye laugh, a sound that echoed through creation. Yet, He saw that some of their mysterious power lay in their duality, in their ability to exist as both two and three.

"Feed us, house us, dress us!" they shouted again. Bondye fed, housed, and dressed them, but it only made them desire more. It was another contradiction, and that was good.

Legba watched the Marassa Jumeaux with quiet amusement, but his attention remained on the crossroads. Meanwhile, Bondye realized something profound.

"There is one Legba," He said, "and there are seven. There are two Marassa, and there are three. This is Vodou, My way—it embraces contradiction."

More Loas came, each born to fill the spaces between Bondye and the living. There were as many Loas as there were beings to perceive them. Each carried their own contradictions, their own paradoxes, existing as reflections of the complexities of creation.

Finally, Bondye rested, retreating with His creation gem. The Loas remained as intermediaries, not entirely divine yet not fully mortal, a buffer between humans and the One We Cannot See. For a long time, Bondye was no longer lonely, and creation continued to unfold in its intricate, contradictory dance.

First Bride of Erzulie

Long ago in Dahomey, a young woman named Daasi captivated anyone who would listen to her extraordinary tales of creation and adventure. She spoke with confidence about how the sun came to hang in the sky, and about an ancient giantess whose tears created the oceans. Word of her stories spread far beyond her village. People traveled great distances to hear her, bringing gifts that made her rich.

Men of all kinds came to make Daasi their wife. There were shiny men of nobility who spoke ancient tongues that could call torrential rain at will. But Daasi smelled bitter sourness in those rains. There were sharp men who used mud cloth to predict coming wars and famine with stunning accuracy. But the mud cloth required the labor of too many tired women who worked until they sometimes dropped from exhaustion. Even the loud chief of Daasi's tribe desired her as one of his wives. But Daasi refused, for she had seen his cruelty and greed too many times.

Out of anger, the chief called his warriors and had them throw her into a dungeon. "You will change your mind after a night in captivity!" he hissed.

In the dungeon, Daasi met many of the chief's other wives, who were sick and starving. She tried to offer them comfort, but she herself was shaking with fear. She fell asleep out of exhaustion and dreamt of a large woman with eyes blazing like fire.

"Resist that greedy chief," said the red-eyed woman. "I will protect you."

"How can I trust you?" Daasi asked. "I will die in here!"

"When you wake, you will see my marking on the dungeon floor," the woman replied. "This is my *vèvè*. When you draw it and offer me something with love, I will mount you, and you will become one of my horses."

"Who are you?" Daasi asked, eager for protection but not believing.

"I am a Loa called Erzulie," said the woman. "And there are as many of me as there are ways to love."

When Daasi awoke in the dungeon, she found the flat symbol of a bloody heart pierced by two blades etched into the dirt floor. She gazed at it in wonder but was soon interrupted. The chief burst in, followed by his warriors.

"Will you marry me now?" he barked.

Daasi refused him a second time.

By the chief's furious command, Daasi was cast into the desert with no water or provisions. She wandered for one day, battered by the winds until she collapsed.

As she lay in the scorched sand, she drew Erzulie's *vèvè* and began to hear distant drums and a song that came in repetitive chants. Remembering, she croaked with her bone-dry throat, "I offer you my life, and my ability to tell stories."

Daasi felt a great, overwhelming pressure and weight on top of her head and many hands gripping her arms, yanking her to her feet. She danced. Her heart filled with boiling water and wine, and she could only see red. She could feel Erzulie holding on and guiding her.

When Daasi awoke, she stood in the center of her village, holding one bloody sword in each of her hands. The chief and his finest warriors lay dead at her feet. The chief's wives, now freed, wept with joy. Dropping the blades, Daasi stood in stunned silence as the villagers bowed to her, calling her their new chief.

Reluctantly, she accepted their praise but gave all the glory to Bondye, the One We Cannot See, who created Erzulie. She made offerings and told stories in the Loa's honor. Erzulie visited Daasi in dreams, sometimes as her bride, sometimes as her mother, and other times as her sister.

"You will wear white and red in my ceremonies," Erzulie said, naming Daasi her high priestess.

Daasi shared Erzulie's words with her people and led them with wisdom and strength. Her tales became legend, and she ruled as a warrior and storyteller whose name endures to this day.

Gens de Couleur

The stage of the Royal Port-Au-Prince Theater was an ocean in the middle of a storm, and Fabienne was like a lone ship cresting its waves. The gawking, powder-faced stares of the blancs in the front and the gens de couleur on the balconies pushed her, threatening to make her buckle under the force. Beneath the thick powder on her skin, carefully applied to lighten the dark patches scattered across her face, her true shade of warm brown hid in shame.

Fabienne swept her arms and bent forward, belting out the words as her white ballroom dress swished under her form. A woman with blue eyes in the ornately decorated gros blanc section gasped and covered her mouth. Who was this mulattress who dared to strut on the stage and sing with such force and fervor? The maestro's piano reached the end of her solo, signaling the moment when Fabienne was supposed to step back and humbly hand the production's attention back to the stars. These petit blancs could not hold a tune or sing anywhere near as well as she could.

Fabienne drew a breath and sustained the note that she was supposed to cut off, even as the piano faltered into the next song. Off to the side of the stage, she could see Duplessi standing up, a caramel-colored face in a sea of white. He drew his hand across his neck once, twice, urging her to get off the stage *now*.

Fabienne felt the attention of the audience, like a burning ray of the sun parting the storm and coating her body. Five hundred pairs of eyes and ears—not counting the men and women sharing the stage—observed her. In that moment of silence when her lungs let go of the note, she met with the blue eyes of the blanc woman in the front row and saw a dark brown spot grow in between those eyes, no bigger than a pea. This spot startled Fabienne and spoke to her, saying, "Oh, sing more. Please sing more."

The blanc woman shot up out of her chair, clapping her hands together and then tumbling forward, blue eyes wide in shock. Fabienne stopped singing then and stepped back, gathering her dress with a small bow as she had been instructed. But the blanc woman with the growing spot on her forehead followed, reaching out for Fabienne and wailing as the crowd gasped.

"Is there a doctor in the audience?!" someone called out, and Fabienne was fleeing backstage as the next song began, her sandaled feet thumping on the wood. Duplessi, from behind the curtains, seized her by the arm, yanking her toward him.

"Wait," Fabienne said, covering her face with her hand because sometimes that made him reconsider hitting her. The blows did not come, and neither did a slew of curses from his rotten, rum-soaked mouth. His grip loosened, and she lowered her hand to see that he was holding a poster. When he spoke, he whispered so that no one could hear him over the singing on the stage.

"Whatever you did out there, it's going to make this theater the most famous venue in the world," Duplessi said, nodding. "You're going to play Nina in a month. Look, that's your name." He unrolled the poster and showed her the printed text, which did indeed have her name and a big drawing of her face on it, alongside words like "magnifique." Of course, Fabienne had to pretend that she could not read.

"I'm... grateful, Monsieur. Thank you." She bowed her head and held it there, unable to accept the reality of what was happening. She thought about the spot on that woman's face and remembered enduring insults from strangers because of her skin discoloration. She had been a child then, crying into her mother's lap, hands clutched around the bronze coins they had earned singing on the streets.

Maman had not comforted her. Instead, she had pinched her ear hard and whispered fiercely, "Stop it. I didn't survive being a slave to raise a crying little girl. I *wish* I had the opportunity you do. If you stop crying, one day your face will be everywhere. In theaters!"

Fabienne sniffled and tried to be strong, but she was not like her mother. "I'm too ugly," she sobbed, and there was a crooning tone in her misery.

Maman wiped away her tears with a calloused thumb. "We're going to see someone who can fix you. And then you'll be able to make more money."

The next night, she had taken Fabienne to the outskirts of the city, to a mambo who listened to Maman's story. She had tried everything, every charm and ointment, to fix what she thought was wrong with Fabienne. The mambo took all of Maman's money and promised a ceremony that would make her daughter's uneven skin tone one uniform shade. Fabienne would become her beautiful little singing mulattress.

Fabienne had stood alone in the middle of the *vèvè*, her small feet bare against the drawn lines of cornmeal. Women danced around her, their white skirts swirling, their bodies moving in time with the drums. Smoke from burning herbs curled thick in the air, making her eyes sting. She had wanted so badly to cry, to run to her mother, to beg to go home. But Maman had been watching her from the shadows, her cool umber face tight with something that did not feel like love.

"Be strong," Maman had hissed. "I gave everything for you. Now sing."

So, Fabienne sang a wordless song pleading for even-toned skin that would lead to theaters and fame and acceptance.

When the air shuddered and the colors of the women bled into each other, when something heavy and old coiled around half of her head and her neck, she knew she had been heard.

Maman Melanj spilled into her mind like oily ink, shifting, reconfiguring, testing.

A thousand skin tones swirled across her body, never staying fixed. She did not seize Fabienne completely. She could not.

"Interesting," the Loa murmured, her form silvery blue, laughter curling in her voice. "You resist me! But you still sing. A stubborn little horse. A strong one!"

Fabienne clenched her fists at her sides but did not stop singing. Even as her voice wavered. Even as the Loa's presence weighed down one side of her skull like a wet shroud.

"You want to be a big singer, little one?" Maman Melanj teased, soft as indigo. "You want to erase these beautiful warm brown patches around your body?"

Fabienne had nodded desperately, had pleaded for the darker spots to disappear, for her skin to be smooth, uniform, pale.

The Loa laughed the humored, amused laugh of an engineer testing a mechanism that had almost worked but still needed adjustments.

"One kind of skin won't get you what you want.," Maman Melanj had said, grinning grass green. "But I will stay around when you sing. This will be *delightful.*"

Fabienne's singing had turned into a feverish shrieking. Maman Melanj had not fixed the patches on her skin and remained buried in her mind since.

Now, as Duplessi stood before her, as the weight of her voice and its consequence settled heavy in her chest, she could feel the Loa's presence again, the whisper of colors pressing down on her.

The rainbow-colored voices rested on top of her head, but Fabienne did not bow to them completely. She let the voices hum, let them wait, let them ache. She had learned something, too. Maman Melanj wanted her because she would not break.

"We'll start rehearsal tomorrow morning." Duplessi rolled up the poster and seemed to want to say something else. Usually, he would chastise her for staying on the stage too long or plant a smelly kiss on her when no one was looking. Now, he just stood there, and Fabienne noticed a spot on his forehead, smaller than the blonde woman's but darker, and it traveled left and right across his brow. Fabienne exited stage left and prayed that he would not follow her.

When Fabienne went outside onto the humid streets of Rue Leclerc, where nègres waited with horses and carriages, she saw Ti Blag pacing back and forth with his hands in his pockets. The mahogany-skinned man jumped up and rushed over to her, casting looks over his shoulder.

"Are you okay?" he asked, embracing her. She inhaled his scent—always rice and beans—and released the breath she had been holding.

"I... I did something,"

"I know," Ti Blag said. "You sang the fuck outta that song."

"Ti Blag..."

"You sang so well the horses were like *wvruhhhhuh*?"

She pushed away from him and held onto his broad arms tight, urging him to stop his perfect equine impression.

"What?" Ti Blag, her joking lover, frowned, his bright grin turning somber in an instant. "Is it that mulattre bastard? Did he hurt you?"

Fabienne shook her head. Duplessi had hurt her, but it wasn't Ti Blag's place to deal with him.

"I did something... to a blanc woman," she said, before trying to explain what had happened.

"That was YOU?" Ti Blag exclaimed, then stifled his sound as another worker walked by. "I saw them dragging some rich bitch outta there, kicking and screaming—"

"Shh," Fabienne said, heart pounding. "I don't know what to do. I feel like I'm going crazy. And I'm going to be playing Nina, I think—"

"Who's Nina?"

Fabienne sighed and tried to explain, but the crowd was applauding during a scene break. She would be expected backstage.

"What is it, Chérie? You can tell me." Ti Blag wouldn't let go of her hand, but she yanked it away, feeling like the lonely ship on the water once more.

"I can't," she said, and went back into the theater.

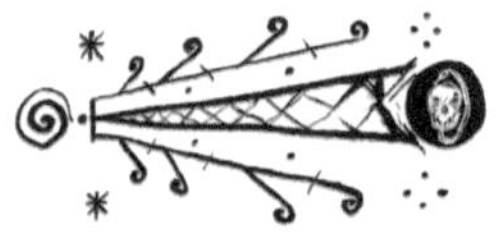

Without wealthy gawking patrons, the theater was a cavern, amplifying every sound. Fabienne stood on the stage, holding her hands on her midriff as Duplessi waved his composition in her face.

"Sing it again with force," he said, even though she had sung the introductory movement four times already. The composition was a blur of dots and lines.

Ships on the waves, Fabienne thought with an old voice that sounded like her mother's, accented with Jamaican Patois-French:

Nègres wit blanc spots, you see dem.

Mulattre with griffe spots—

Duplessi's snapping fingers cut off her invading thoughts. "Now. Again!"

Fabienne poured her heart out to the empty theater, and the nègres sweeping up the patrons' trash stopped and looked at her. Fabienne could feel the members of the troupe on the balcony pausing, along with that hot feeling of the sun cooking her. She could not hold the wave back. She was just a small ship. To hold it back would collapse her lungs. She pushed through and completed the aria, holding up her left hand. The pianist, a gros blanc man, held up his left hand too, playing only with his right, looking up and around in shock. Two spots blossomed on his forehead and his neck as he tumbled away from the piano, gurgling.

Duplessi jerked his hand for the nègres to come over and help hold the man down while he had a seizure, boots clattering on the floor.

"Go get a doctor, you fools!" the theater director spat, trying to clear a circle.

The pianist's eyes rolled in his head and fixed on Fabienne as she watched, her heart pounding. The brown-black spots grew on his face, discoloring his skin and keeping pace with her heartbeat. He grunted something that sounded like "Mmnn Mnnnj," then snatched Duplessi's conductor baton from his jacket and stabbed it into his eyes and throat.

Nègre servants swarmed at the right distance and cried out with the requisite amount of concern, but it was an excited crying out, the same as Fabienne's. She could not look away, not even as a doctor came later to observe the corpse. Her heart pounded with fearful clarity; she knew now that she had caused the woman's madness before, the pianist's violent death now. The spots were her doing, a debt to Maman Melanj she could no longer avoid.

The Loa's voice dripped into her ear, a tangy yellow.

"Careful, now. You strain against your harness. Every horse must learn its limits. In time, I'll mix many like you, every soul a unique soup. My future horses will learn control from your pain."

Fabienne grasped at her powdered neck, trembling. "What more do you want?" she whispered. The Loa only smiled, distant yet unmistakable, pulling invisible threads tighter around Fabienne's heart.

"You see now," the Loa purred, warm and slick against the back of Fabienne's skull. "We are bound, my little songbird. Every note, every breath. You sing for both of us!"

"Go home," Duplessi said to the actors, wiping blood on his jacket and shaking. Before Fabienne could make it out the door, she heard him bark at her: "Rehearsal tonight. Nothing will stop this show. Nothing!"

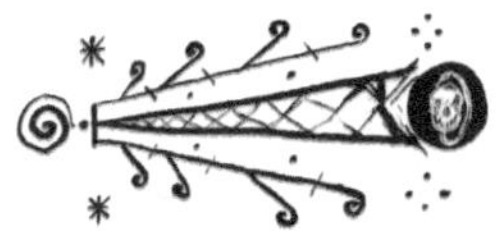

"Was it the same blanc pianist who said you shouldn't be allowed onstage?" Ti Blag rolled onto his side, nearly pushing Fabienne off the tiny bed in the corner of his shack.

"Yeah, him," she said, elbowing him for more room, which caused him to giggle. It seemed like everything caused him to giggle. "I'm scared. It's not funny."

Ti Blag traced her cheek softly, fingertips lifting faint layers of powder from her skin. "You don't need all this," he whispered, his voice low and serious. "Why hide yourself, Chérie mwen?"

She looked away, heart heavy. "They'd never accept me if they saw what I really look like."

Ti Blag frowned slightly, his thumb brushing along her jaw where the powder was thinnest. Beneath it, a patch of warm brown peeked through.

"Maman Melanj didn't make your skin one color when you were a child, did she?"

Fabienne shook her head, jaw set with irritation at the Loa who still lived inside of her.

"Doesn't matter. I accept you. And one day, so will everyone else," he murmured, gently wiping more powder away and revealing more the darker patches of skin she had tried to conceal.

"You are beautiful, Chérie. Don't let them tell you otherwise."

Ti Blag planted kisses on her exposed neck and collarbone. The sensation of his mouth felt distant, and she looked at his skin and wondered if she could infect him, too, with whatever was inside of her.

Fabienne got out of his bed and hunted for her undergarments and shift.

"Something's coming, Chérie. No more slavery and no more begging for a way to survive," he said.

"Not this revolution shit again. Spare me. I'm talking about my life here!"

"Then think about *my* life." Ti Blag stood and closed the distance between them. The man was large and towered over her, the branding scar of his previous owner calloused on his chest. Just like the one Maman had shown her. Fabienne flapped her hand at him and tried to look away, and he took her chin. "I was born a slave but worked my way to freedom, scrounging every coin I could, learning how to read in secret. Now I have to work driving horses back and forth across this city, shoveling shit every goddamn day to make someone else richer."

Fabienne pulled away from his touch and looked away, rolling her eyes at this familiar rant. Next, he would talk about slavery.

Ti Blag continued. "We outnumber the blancs on this island by far. Slaves and free men, maroons…"

"Who's *we*?" Fabienne asked with a smirk that she knew would annoy him. "The gens de couleur? Mulattres? Griffes? Sacatras? Mameloucs?"

"That's all fake!" He stomped back and forth, gesturing passionately in that way she found endearing and insufferable all at once. "Those are all words that the blancs in France made up to make us *think* we're different just because of our skin color!"

Fabienne sighed. "They're never going to free all of the slaves, and if they did, I'd have much more competition in the theaters."

Ti Blag clapped his hands together. "Okay then, think about this. Duplessi has been taking your money for years, and you *know* everyone else gets paid more than you. Don't you want what's fair?"

She looked away, not wanting to think about how she was treated and robbed daily at the theater. Ti Blag caressed her shoulder.

"I've been in contact with Toussaint, Chérie… Transporting messages and preparing his horses for missions. He has plans to eliminate slavery and free us. I've told him about you, and he's interested. You could help—"

"No," she replied while kissing his calloused hand. "You don't understand what it's like onstage. What's on my shoulders and in my heart." Her mother had not understood either, no matter what she thought.

"I do understand."

Their lovemaking was panicked and fierce, like he was trying to convince her with his body to join him and his foolish rebels.

After, Ti Blag asked her to sing to him, his voice soft, finally free of jokes. So, she did. She sang a portion of the song contained in *Nina* that she would have to practice later. He watched with teary eyes, whispering to her and his humble shack. "Your voice is like cuisine for my ears." Though the compliment was sincere, Fabienne rolled her eyes and turned away. It was different to hear it from someone who she loved and cared for.

Ti Blag must have known that she was tender-hearted in this moment, because he continued in his serious tone. "We could leave the city and find Rosette. And your little niece."

Fabienne barked out a dry laugh in disbelief at his half-baked plan. What a naïve man her lover was! She clamped her mouth shut and shoved him playfully.

"I need to go back to the theater," Fabienne said. She tried to get up, but now Ti Blag seized her by the hips with his strong worker's hands. The thought of staying was tempting, but she didn't want him to think that he could control her or get her to change her mind. She cast a look at him that made him loosen his grip.

Maman Melanj chuckled in imitation of Ti Blag as Fabienne gathered her dress and headwrap, fleeing his shack before she second-guessed herself.

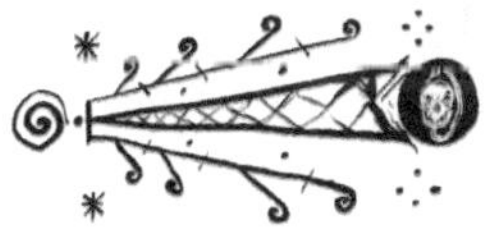

The next three weeks smeared by like the hastily scrawled spots on Duplessi's scrolls. She read the *Nina* script in secret and practiced onstage for many sweaty, foot-cramp-inducing hours. Duplessi's only mention of the catastrophic events she caused was that the actors needed to focus more.

"I need more *passion* if you're going to be the lead here," he shouted one afternoon, though no one was more passionate or hardworking than she was. Fabienne was always the lead, no matter what production she was on! She remained silent and stomped away backstage in the middle of practice, causing the entire theater company to stop and stare. Duplessi followed, trying to seize her hand, and she pushed him away with disgust, tasting a sour tang in her mouth.

"What has gotten into you?" he asked, eyes wide and bloodshot.

Fabienne pressed her palms to her temples to hold back the pulsing green tingle of heat and pain building inside of her. "You never yell at anyone else that way," she squeaked out—hardly the powerful outburst she'd hoped for.

Duplessi recoiled as if he had been slapped.

"I just want to-to be treated like I'm the lead. I deserve better." Fabienne's throat closed and she shook, looking down at her feet. She was weak, throwing everything away just because she had been yelled at.

Nosy members of the theater company poked their heads from around the curtain to watch, and Fabienne felt like she was even smaller now, wanting to disappear. Duplessi's jaw worked as he hunted in his jacket and pulled out a poster. His words came as softly as hers had. "Perhaps it's best that I changed a few things in the poster design."

He offered the new poster of *Nina* to Fabienne, and she took it with her trembling, powder-coated hands.

The main image on the poster was of a petit blanc actress in the theater company, in Nina's makeup and dress. The woman couldn't hold a tune and was barely an understudy to Fabienne on her best day. "You're... *replacing* me?" The room swam with her tears and the nausea building up within her.

Duplessi's voice sounded like it was coming from far away. "You'll still play Nina, but I wanted to address some of the public's concerns."

"The opening night is already sold out," Fabienne muttered, looking over the poster repeatedly. Her name had been removed as well. "I'm not on here."

"This is the opportunity of a lifetime," Duplessi said, trying to put a hand on the poster to take it back, but Fabienne wouldn't let go. She clenched it, squeezed until it tore.

"That's coming out of your pay!" he snapped, leaving the area. "I don't care what sort of crazy ideas you have rolling around in your little head. I'm the director, not you. Take five, then I want you back onstage!"

Fabienne quivered, slamming her palms against her temples again, trying to hold back the waves of red-tinged thoughts.

They thought she was too ugly to be onstage. They knew about the makeup. She couldn't trick them into thinking she was a light-skinned mulattre, after all. No, someone had sabotaged her, one of the other actresses. Her mother would have been so disappointed in her. No. No. No—

Maman Melanj came slinking to the front of her awareness, sing-song voice coming out creamy pink. "Still mad about your life, my dear horse? When are you going to *really* let me in? We'll show them what happens when you *really* sing!"

"No," Fabienne whispered, hunting for a mirror to check her makeup. Her skin looked clammy, and she had clearly been about to cry, but she would not leave practice early. Maman Melanj sucked her teeth and watched.

Fabienne went through with rehearsals because she was a professional and had been raised by a woman who was born a slave. She sang with passion and endured the stares and the laughs because her mother had endured much worse. But as she performed, she imagined the multicolored spots from before—growing, spreading—and that carried her. The colors were balm for the rage building within her.

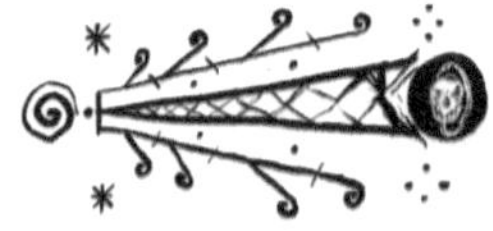

She told Ti Blag later in his shack. He washed off the powder from her skin carefully, then held her as she cried. He did not judge, telling her that she was beautiful, singing to her, but his voice was so bad she told him to stop, laughing and so grateful that this silly man could show her that she could still laugh.

"I'll leave the city with you before it gets too bad," she said, and he seemed to grow lighter in his elation as she continued, holding his face in her hands. "But I'm doing it for me, not for you or Toussaint or to free slaves. I'll help because I can't take this anymore, understand?"

He nodded, though Fabienne could never be sure that he really understood. Such a naïve, reliable man. Together, they planned what would come next.

The show would go on, and Maman Melanj would be taking the stage with her.

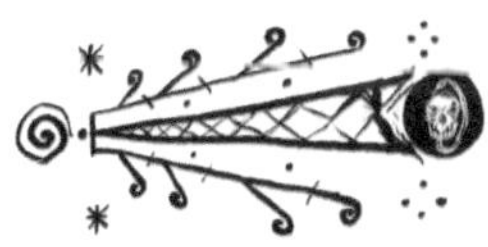

On the night of the performance, twice as many patrons came and packed the theater, all to see the actress who had been onstage when a woman went insane. Those who only heard about it wanted to see for themselves. Ti Blag stood by the back entrance of the theater with his horse and carriage, and did not make eye contact with Fabienne, as they had planned. She threaded her way through members of the theater troupe. Actors pretended like she wasn't there, like she wasn't the lead in this production.

Fabienne found her small corner backstage where she could check her makeup and sang softly to a hand-held mirror. "I'm ready for you."

The reply came from inside her skull, thick as golden molasses. "I've been waiting a long time for this."

Fabienne's heart began to gallop in her chest. Though she had expected to hear Maman Melanj, she had not expected to feel the thrill that mixed with her usual jitters before any performance.

The Loa was already there, breathing with her, watching through her eyes, waiting, always waiting.

"Are you ready?"

Duplessi's hand pressed against the small of her back. Fabienne startled out of her conversation with Maman Melanj, inhaling sharply, realizing he was inspecting her makeup.

His gaze flicked across her face, slow, calculating. His lips pressed together.

I don't care, she thought for the first time.

The powder was uneven now. The warm brown patches Maman Melanj had never entirely erased peeked through—the secret she had hidden from him for years.

Fabienne's stomach twisted. Would he comment? Would he try to drag her back and demand an explanation?

I don't care; I'm going out on that stage and we're going to show them all what I can do.

Duplessi turned her toward the stage. Whatever was happening to her skin, it would have to wait. The show must go on.

Fabienne forced her lips into a smile and nodded as they went backstage, where the orchestra played her introduction to the world.

She stood behind the thick red velvet curtains, holding her hands on her midriff, breathing in and out, half-cursing Ti Blag for pulling her into the dangerous machinations of the free nègres and slaves of this cursed colony. But wasn't she already inside another set of hands? Wasn't she already being pulled?

"Go on," Maman Melanj murmured, her voice woven into every breath Fabienne took. "Let's see how far we can take this together."

The violins and piano drowned out these thoughts, and Fabienne was once again a ship launching itself onto the impossible waves.

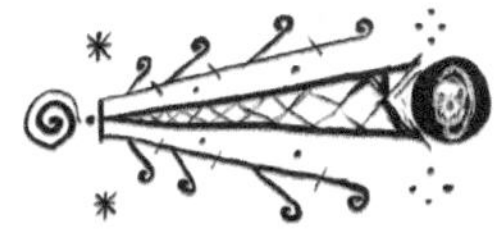

The stage of the Royal Port-Au-Prince Theater was an ocean of eyes and ears, and Fabienne was a lone ship bringing a hurricane in her lungs. She had been supposed to go out onstage arm in arm with her co-star, a blanc man, but he collapsed as soon as she looked at him, writhing on the ground. She proceeded out onto the stage and crested the wave of the overture as it attacked the auditorium, crashing into a feverish pace that slammed in time with her pounding heart.

Fabienne swung her arms, bending forward and back to swallow up the bodies in the theater. The gros blancs in the gilded chairs of the front bent to follow her attention. Spots grew on their faces and necks and hands, then spread in between them, traveling like clouds. The orchestra kept playing as if possessed, and the conductor jerked and waved his baton wide-eyed, looking at the stick as if it were out of his control.

Duplessi watched from the side of the stage, mouth agape and frozen rigid.

Fabienne cried out with a great bellow that felt like vomiting generations of misery. The vibrations rose and scattered over the crowd in the dimly lit theater. Duplessi's light-brown face blossomed into a sharp splatter of browns, reds, and purples. He shrieked in the same key as her singing.

How lovely, she thought at the loathsome man, *so much passion! It's your night!*

A quarteron mistress up in the gens de couleur section cackled as she scratched and scratched her arms, which flicked between a light and dark complexion.

The theater decoration behind her erupted into flames, a black spot eating into a carefully painted background resembling Ancient Athens. Ti Blag had ignited it like she had told him to. Fabienne could hear a distant clattering and struggle behind her, but her attention remained on the swaying, changing crowd. Duplessi slapped his face repeatedly and climbed his way onto the stage, jerking forward as if he had forgotten how to dance. The orchestra matched his movements, continuing the ornate stylings of the ouverture but incorporating the maddening cries from the crowd and the exploding cinders overhead.

A heavy, warm feeling coated her wrapped hair and dripped down over her scalp and into her heart, like melted candle wax. Only it was crawling inside of her body and mixing there, telling her everything she needed to know, and how to move. The feeling burst with the colors of a rainbow, swirling in circular waves, directing her to move and to keep singing.

"Oh, keep playing!" Fabienne's alto carried the words to the orchestra, and she had not forgotten how to move. Duplessi dove to stop her, and she pirouetted out of his way so that he fell on his face. She brought down her arm in a hard line across his body, and the colors of his skin split and stretched, making him moan and thrash against the stage.

A wooden pillar dropped from above, seemingly from heaven and aflame, and smashed a row of gros blancs. Ti Blag tore through the burning backdrop, chased by a cluster of actors screaming words Fabienne could not pay attention to, not now.

"We need to get out of here!" Ti Blag shouted at Fabienne to be heard over the music, clearly nervous onstage with all those eyes on him. He swiped with a machete at the group of blanc actors approaching him, their skin changing rapidly. "God, these people are ugly!"

"...Ti Blag, my love, brought to me by wind and chain..." Fabienne crooned in verse. She slowed, bowing, and Ti Blag gave another swipe at his pursuers. The orchestra's sounds died, leaving only the coughs and dying gasps of the audience as music.

"Uh... that's nice and everything, but we need to go now!"

"Not yet," Fabienne sang. "The blood has not yet set!" The rainbow bristled inside of her with a hot, feverish glee.

Ti Blag stomped on Duplessi's back when he tried to approach her and cut down anyone else who attempted the same, coughing from the growing smoke. The colorful crowd sucked in the smoke and dropped, or they fought each other at Fabienne's slightest whim. Duplessi thrashed and moaned under her, shifting in colors that blossomed on him like a thousand butterflies.

Fabienne sang. "White with black spots... mamelouc with griffe spots..." Then she coughed, suddenly pulled into the reality of the moment. Ti Blag's hand reached out to her through the smoke and pulled her towards cleaner air. Another hand tugged at her leg. Duplessi's face was a grotesque mixture of colors and patterns that swirled in and out of his skin. "Mamannn..." he groaned through a mouth of foam. "Mamannn Melan-nj..."

"What the fuck is that?" Ti Blag groaned and moved to hack the grasping limb away, but Fabienne stilled her lover's machete.

"Not him," she said. There was no time to question it. She jerked her leg away from the crawling monstrosity and followed Ti Blag out into the night, where a different kind of chaos unfolded.

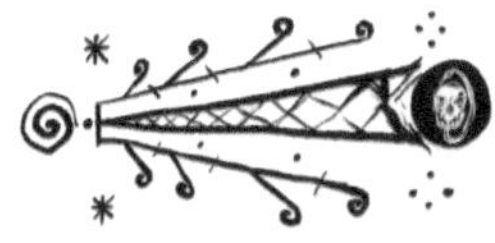

The streets of Port-au-Prince ran with fire and blood. Fabienne and Ti Blag hurried as best they could through the crowds of nègres and gens de couleur. Zombie Duplessi followed them, keeping pace at a loping gait, switching color at a nauseating cadence. He snarled and snapped at any who approached, save for Ti Blag, whom he also seemed to despise down in his bones. Just a look from Fabienne, though, would make him pause.

"Relax." Ti Blag chuckled nervously despite himself.

All Zombie Duplessi could say was "Maman Melanj" in different ways.

They got out of the city in Ti Blag's horse-drawn carriage. Fabienne ordered Zombie Duplessi to get into the back so he wouldn't be seen, and she and Ti Blag rode up front.

"You did it," Ti Blag said, coated in sweat and laughing in the moonlight. "He didn't think you'd join his cause, but I knew you'd come around! You're my Chérie, I told him!"

"Who?" Fabienne mopped sweat and soot from her face, looking over at Ti Blag, whose smile faltered.

"Toussaint!" Ti Blag's grip tightened on the reins. The mention of the man's name made her feel a sharp stab of cold in her jaw.

"I told you already, I didn't do it for him."

"I know you think he's going to bring slavery back. That's not true."

Fabienne thumped her fist against her thigh. "And what about me? What if *I* want to bring slavery back—what then?" The words had come out of her from some hateful place that wanted to make him shut up, and she instantly felt a pang of regret. Zombie Duplessi moaned from inside the carriage, like an attack dog sensing danger.

It's okay, she thought, *you'll never have to attack him.* She hoped that would always be true, and that Ti Blag's allegiance would remain with her.

They rode in silence the rest of the way to the village where she grew up, passing rebels and bandits who somehow knew not to test them. Perhaps it was the look in her eyes, coated with the knowledge of what she could do when the storm inside of her grew too strong.

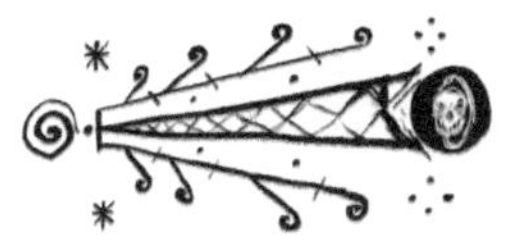

Morning time in the salty-aired seaside village of Plaisance was just as it had been when she had left eleven years back. It had taken them a slow day's journey to get here, and now her sister, Rosette, came running with a small child in tow. A girl—Fabienne's niece called Maria—hid behind her mother's leg.

"Ro?" Fabienne dropped out of the carriage's seat without poise and embraced her sister, hugging her tight and smearing her with mud and soot and dried blood. They held each other at arm's length and laughed with the disbelief of two women who should not have been able to make it in this world.

"We heard what happened. Come on. Let's get you cleaned up." Rosette took her by the shoulder and led her down a short hill towards the smell of boiled banan and djiri a poi.

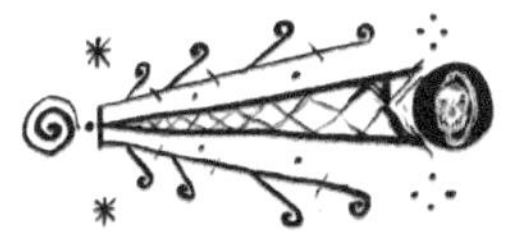

Fabienne woke to the sound of Maria singing, and a familiar sound of clanging wooden spoons against a pot. The smell of hot mais moulen and savory garlic with pork. She was in a small, unadorned shack. Rosette stirred the contents of the pot and handed Maria a pile of green beans to sort.

Ti Blag came through the doorway, wearing a bicorn hat and blue coat. He removed his hat and bowed to Rosette and the child, then went to Fabienne's bedside and took her hands.

"How are you feeling?" he asked, and she wished for the funny version of him.

"Hungry," she said and sat up.

"Slavery is finished," Ti Blag said as a smile began to curl at the corners of his mouth.

"The theater?" she asked. He shook his head.

"The blancs?"

He shook his head again, this time with a full grin that went up into his eyes and beyond, to that other place where his dreams of freedom lived.

"There's someone here who wants to talk to you." Ti Blag patted her hands. She looked down at her skin, light brown against his mahogany.

"Who?" she asked.

"Toussaint." He said the name with a whisper, as if it were a spirit.

"Toussaint?" Maria repeated, and Rosette shushed her.

Fabienne looked at little Maria and her green beans. "Do you want help sorting those? Bring them. Let's go outside."

Fabienne got up and left the shack, taking her niece with her. Ti Blag followed, huffing like he always did when he was annoyed. "Chérie. He wants us to find others like you," he said. "He can give us arms and protection. Land, he says."

Fabienne sat with Maria, the green beans between them, and showed her how to sort them. "Thank you for helping me," she said to Ti Blag. The man opened his mouth and closed it. Then he walked away, flapping his hand in the air.

Maria's hands were small and delicate, but she snapped green beans with quick precision. Just like Fabienne's mother had taught her and Rosette. The child put the darker ones into a separate pile, though they were still edible.

"Why do you put the other ones away?" Fabienne asked, recalling how she had done the same thing as a little girl.

"The dark ones have spots on them. Look, oui." Maria held up the beans for just a moment. Green, dark green, and too-bright green.

Green.

Green with black spots.

Green with white spots.

Fabienne took the dark beans from the discard pile and mixed them in with the lighter green beans. "They're still good. Your maman won't be mad. Trust me."

Maria smiled a bright smile that contained innocence and wonder.

"I heard you singing back there," Fabienne said with a smile of her own. "Can you sing for me again?"

Maria sang, with a voice that was untrained but pure in its naïvety. This was a girl who would not be snatched up and made to sing for free under the guise of tutelage and prosperity. She paused suddenly, reaching to touch Fabienne's cheek. "Why do you put on powder, Tante Fabienne? You're beautiful here." The child pointed to the exposed patches of darker skin. Fabienne felt warmth bloom in her heart and embraced her niece.

"I know, Chérie," Fabienne whispered, feeling free for the first time. "I know now." Fabienne sang with her, picking up her tune and elevating it, wishing to envelop the girl with safety she had never known. They sang and sorted beans, throwing away the rotten ones but keeping all the colors together. Mixed.

Up and in the distance, past a cluster of banan trees, a figure swayed and groaned in time with her singing. Zombie Duplessi watched, mumbling, "Maman Melanj," with a hunger that would never again be sated. Fabienne lifted her chin and let the voices inside her spill free, singing, at last, with every color she had ever been.

Grief in Reverse

D r. Jean-Jacques Placide climbed carefully through the Vèvè-Net's microscopic simulation of Samedi-Immunodeficiency Virus-15 (SHIV-15). The virus was a spherical lattice of white light against a black world, each node pulsing like a breath, shifting as the virus replicated and spread, mapping itself onto Patient 304's body in the real world, who was fighting for her life many levels above.

The Gran Komansman of 2002 had changed everything when Placide was a boy. The events of that day rewrote the fundamental connections between humans, Loas, and technology. Here, inside the Vèvè-Net, those fractures were most visible. But it hadn't given him the power to save his mother from SHIV-1, which had infected her with the Bad Sickness.

Dr. Placide whispered through the tall oak mask affixed to his skull, "You hurt won't I..." To unspeak in reverse-transcriptase required a precise inversion of breath, words, and sometimes grammar.

A backward whimper came from ahead, deep in SHIV-15's core. Placide picked towards the sound, panting.

"What was that sound?" asked Dr. Louis Duplessi, his mentor, who was patrolling the higher levels of the simulation, like a captain radioing a tethered deep-sea diver. "It was like a song."

"It's just a glycoprotein burst," Placide said, feeling embarrassment burn in his chest as he hurried to grab protein branches. SHIV-15 shrank away from his close inspection, losing its heat and energy. The multicolored strands flickered and dimmed. The young doctor's fingers moved like a forager's through the dying light as he hunted, isolating the viral protein strands, twisting them, reading them. There was a problem with how SHIV-15 was shutting down.

It was afraid of him.

Dr. Placide's mind worked at double speed, aided by his mask as he played and replayed the whimper. It *had* spoken to him, pleaded the way many other viruses had—just never this clearly.

"You hurt won't I," he repeated, noticing the whimpering sound coming from a fungal ribosome. He snatched and squeezed it hard, baring his teeth. A sudden, high-pitched shriek rippled through the simulated environment and pierced his ears.

"You understand to want I!" Duplessi shrieked back as SHIV-15's code unraveled like a frayed thread, each node around him a dying star blinking out. The virus was unpleading in reverse transcriptase. The sound made him shake with an anger that threatened to crush him.

SHIV-1 was a beautiful, complex virus that had been used as a bioweapon to kill so many. It had broken the body down and left it open to infections long cured. Placide's mother, Ednice, had been broken down by this bioweapon in the years before the Gran Komansman—when the Bad Sickness was a death sentence with no possible pardon, even if you were Haitian and had access to the best medicine in the Pan-Caribbean African Union.

SHIV-15 was one of SHIV-1's many descendants, an infantile offshoot that was nowhere near as beautiful, nor as deadly. Dr. Placide snapped the final sequence for data extraction from this strain. Numbers flooded the Vèvè-Net interface through his mask, a cascade of confirmation data, diagrams unraveling into a final sequence that would auto-manufacture a vaccine up above.

Dr. Duplessi's voice cut through the loud, backward sobbing of SHIV-15.

"Okay, come out of there," said Duplessi, preparing to pull the deep-sea diver from the bottom of a treacherous ocean.

Placide climbed out of SHIV-15 and felt himself growing. As everything around him shrank, he saw the lights inside of SHIV-15 and its countless clones dying, each with frightened sobs and unapologies in their viral-language that he had only recently deciphered.

Dr. Placide listened with some pleasure to the dying virus family's reaction, panicking in its own incomprehensible way. Placide's breathing was steady, controlled. But beneath the mask, his pulse surged. There was a rush that was almost primal in nature—watching something so small, so insidious, so powerful break itself because of him.

That's it, he sneered with triumph at SHIV-15, *I'm not scared of your kind. You will try to come back, but I will enter you again. You will know what it feels like to just want to die, but that will only be the start. I'm not finished with you.*

The Vèvè-Net shifted, pulling Placide upward, drawing him back to his normal scale, and leaving behind the dying echoes of SHIV-15's last fragments.

As the surgical interface collapsed, he could still hear the trillions of viral clones apologizing in reverse.

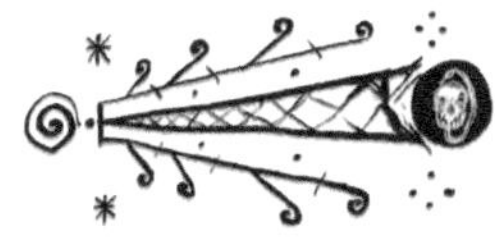

Coming out of the Vèvè-Net was like filling his lungs with cold, sterile air. With every breath, the blackness of the void gained color, and the lights melted away as the numbers and diagrams and the knowledge of the spiky virus-shaped plastic model in his pocket fell away.

"Merci, Chaquepana," Dr. Placide said, offering the discovery of SHIV-15's vulnerability to the healing Loa who owned the majority share, 21.3%, of his soul. The Loa regarded his discovery with little more than a shrug from Lòt bòa, where his kind supposedly lived and made their deals.

I'm not scared of your kind, either, the young doctor thought in the millisecond it took for the Loa to release him back into his body from the Vèvè-Net.

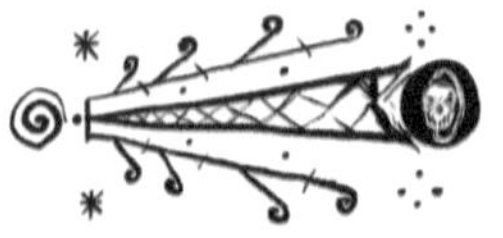

The sterile smell of antiseptic came first, then the feeling of the red oak wood mask that clung to his sweaty face. Dr. Placide was lying on a table in Dr. Duplessi's operating theater, a semicircle of Vodouite doctors watching from ascending benches above. They burst into applause, some cheering and standing.

Dr. Placide nodded and waved reluctantly at the crowd above, sitting up. The Gran Komansman had transformed medical practice, turning viral research into a form of spiritual warfare against those who had almost ended PCAU from the inside.

"You did it again," Dr. Duplessi said beside him, helping the young man remove the tall wooden mask. "Good job, kid." The senior doctor's voice carried its usual calm authority, but there was a tautness beneath that made Placide pause despite the cheering.

Beside him, Patient 304 stirred underneath a sani-quilt as a group of doctors and nurses checked her vitals.

"Is she stable?" Placide asked, keeping his tone neutral as he swung his legs off the table. Dr. Duplessi glanced down at the purple Soleil PlayKid in his hands, scanned the readouts, and gave a confident nod.

The young doctor lifted his head as if he wanted to say something, but Duplessi made his way out of the operating theater and upstairs towards the silence of the staff corridor.

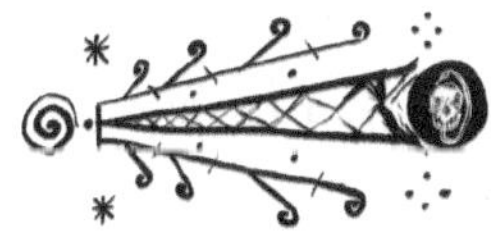

Placide polished his mask in his office while a loud celebration thumped on the other side of the locked door. There was plenty to celebrate. The latest strain of SHIV would be cured, making future strains much easier to detect, and it was because of his actions. Jean-Jacques Placide, the twenty-eight-year-old wunderkind of a world remade by the Gran Komansman.

Adam tell should I, he thought so suddenly that he clenched his fists, pushing the reverse thought away.

A knock on his door made him stiffen up and look over his shoulder.

"Sorry. Busy," he said.

Dr. Duplessi's voice came from the other side. "You ain't doing shit. Lemme in, just for a second."

Placide let out a breath and got up to unlock the door. The man who had taken him under his wing eight years ago had not aged a day, save for the many gray hairs on the sides of his head. He was looking down at his purple Soleil PlayKid, thumbs and fingers twiddling at the infamous game console that was so much more.

Placide went back to his desk and sat down, pretending to look at his computer screen. Duplessi's words came out slower than usual, and his fingers stopped poking at the PlayKid. "I know you wanna be alone. But I needed to tell you that I'm proud of you."

Placide threaded his hands together and hung his head. He did not expect the words to hit him so hard, but it took the breath out of him. He felt like the man was the only person who could see him—*really* see him. And yet...

He opened his mouth to say something, like *thank you*, or *you're the closest thing I ever had to a dad*, or *I wouldn't be anything without you*, but instead he said nothing.

Duplessi continued, having predicted that the young man would stall out. "Tomorrow's case is going to be different. I want you to look carefully at this."

Placide's computer chimed, and he was all too eager to sit up and engage with it. Anything but having to tell his mentor what was really on his mind. Patient 178 was an older white man, aged and gaunt—like most soufri who drifted through the world in a perpetual state of bewilderment, trapped in endless mental loops, constantly reliving the moment they lost everything to the PCAU and the Vodouites. Their minds seemed stuck, like damaged recording devices replaying the same traumatic fragment of a war they almost won, unable to reconcile their former significance with their current irrelevance.

Placide froze, eyes bulging with sudden recognition.

"He's presenting with a novel, viral form of dementia that's been popping up in some of Erzulie's mercy shelters," said Duplessi, pulling the information with ease from his PlayKid. "Neurological deterioration, memory mutation... It's a mess." His voice carried a clinical detachment. "This virus replaces memories after the typical plaque protein erosion. Builds a false reality inside the patient's mind. They exist in two places at once: here in the real world, and somewhere else they can't fully describe. Some kind of dream version of their past. But it gets weirder. We think the patients can communicate with each other."

"*Through* the virus?" Placide asked, narrowing his eyes. On instinct, he reached into his pocket and grasped the spiky plastic model of the virus he carried, squeezing until it bit into his palm. The hard, sharp pain kept him from shaking as he looked at the old patient's face.

"I know. It's dezod," Duplessi said. He pointed his PlayKid at the image of Patient 178. "You know who he is, right?"

Placide answered with a mixture of historical contempt and the detachment of a perfect student. "Minority party leader Casper Langley, the self-proclaimed general of the American Resistance Army. The poor fuckers who almost managed to take down the PCAU. *Almost*."

Duplessi stopped clicking on his device. "Given his connection to your history, if you don't want this case, you don't have to—"

"I can do it," Placide shot back, with a bit more force than he expected. "It's not gonna be a problem for me," he added to try to soften the reaction, unclenching the spiked ball in his pocket. "And, besides, Langley and the ARA always try to take credit for the Bad Sickness, but it was all Papa Samedi's idea anyway."

Duplessi pressed his lips together, looking around as if they were being watched. "You want to be very careful when you say things like that. It's better if you don't talk about him."

But the young doctor didn't truly understand why it was so controversial to talk about Papa Samedi and what he did. SHIV was his namesake, after all. To bring his point back, he repeated himself. "I'll treat him. I can do it."

Duplessi closed the distance between them and put a gentle hand on the young man's shoulder. "I know you can. But if you get in there tomorrow and find that it's too much, tell me. We'll get someone else on it. And you know you can talk to me anytime. Cynthia and I would love to have you over for dinner. Denise is always asking for you."

Placide nodded, wanting to be alone. Duplessi got the hint and pulled his hand back. As he went back out the door, Placide's words spilled out of him.

"Sometimes I just think about how everyone just let my mother suffer and die. No one did anything to help—"

"That's not true," Duplessi said, putting his hand on the doorknob. "We all lost people. A lot more could have been done, yeah, but there were always people who cared."

Placide drummed his fingers on the table, unsure of what else he wanted to say, or how to articulate it. That wasn't his strong suit.

"Your brother cared," his mentor said.

"He *left* after our aunt took us in," Placide hissed. "He left me with *her*." Visions came to him then, of how his mother's sister had made them suffer. Sometimes he understood why Adam had left. But mostly, it created an aching wound inside of him, raw and unable to heal.

A long moment passed. Someone outside was singing along to a song.

"You want the door open or closed?" Duplessi asked. This made them both laugh together for a while.

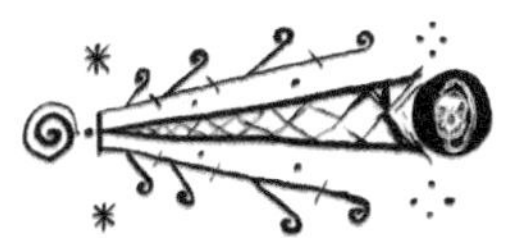

The Ryde Jean-Jacques took to his childhood home was a blur of streetlights and static. Memories flickered like the fragmented Loa power unleashed during the Gran Komansman—fractal, but potent. He barely remembered pulling the mask over his face when he was standing before the small, unremarkable building that had once housed too many families who could barely afford to live in Dessalines.

He owned the building now, a testament to the strange opportunities that emerged from catastrophe. The Bad Sickness had torn apart everything he knew, leaving him and Adam as orphans in a world harder to endure. He had left for medical school and drifted until Duplessi found him. Until the Vèvè-Net exposed something in him—a healing potential that transcended the ordinary.

Through his mask, Jean-Jacques looked at the window where he and his mother had once lain, her body already consumed by an illness unlike anything the world had seen. Back then, before the Gran Komansman, healing from something like the Bad Sickness seemed impossible. Now, Placide was a perfect tool crafted against the kinds of entities that had taken her life.

The Vèvè-Net coated his consciousness, a digital landscape where memory and possibility intertwined. He summoned two constructs: Patient 178— "General"

Langley in his destitute state—and the memory of his mother.

Within Langley's construct, a memory played on a horrific loop:

"No," Langley shouted in a bunker as he stabbed frantically at the datapad that was supposed to give him control over the last geographical targets of the virus. Nothing happened. Outside, his brothers in arms were being gunned down by the PCAU bastards. "This wasn't the *deal!*" He flung the datapad at the wall, where it crunched. He paced around. "You said it was going to *work*! You sold us out!"

Something small and as vast as SHIV itself replied, coming through the speakers in Langley's bunker. It spoke with a deep, hoarse voice that everyone knew. Papa Samedi's.

"...You're... right..." the voice said. "...That was not... the deal..."

Langley took out his service pistol and jammed the barrel into his mouth.

"...I may have lost... but you're losing with me..." Papa Samedi laughed a million croaking laughs, and the general, now sobbing, pulled the trigger and felt free for just a splinter of a second as the bullet carved away his brain.

But the memory fractured, repeating, and he was back. Sometimes the words changed. Sometimes he was standing in a congressional hall, urging people in the minority political party to join him. Sometimes in a sterile medical room. Sometimes the walls melted, and he was speaking to laughing shadows shaped like the Gasons Samedi, Papa Samedi's personal guerilla army.

"...I may have lost... but you're losing with me..." The multi-voice in the speaker croaked.

"Where am I? Someone help me, please—" The bunker's gray walls melted as he tapped at the datapad again, looking like his current gaunt self as it told him just how many people would die in the resistance because of him.

"Make it stop!"

The memory was a shattered mirror, each fragment reflecting a different moment, a different terror. The virus had turned his recollection into a looping nightmare.

Larger than life, impossible to save, the general's fractured memory haunted the edges of Dr. Placide's vision, alongside the memory of his mother. Both were trapped in their own impossible moments.

"I will save this man," he whispered, the words a promise and a prayer. "For Ednice Regis, mama mwen. Because that's what she would have wanted."

A croaking echo replied through the darkness—sticky, insistent. "...My mother... died *too*..." The voice was familiar. It was Papa Samedi, the boy who became a doctor, and then a dictator, and then a world-scale force of nature. The voice felt spiky like the plastic virus Placide carried in his pocket and cut through his intentions—questioning, challenging. It made Placide's heart hammer against his ribcage, and he tried to take off his mask but found that it would not come off.

The voice continued. "...I could... teach you how to... get what you *really* want..."

That voice knew him, and whatever was inside of it knew him, perhaps better than anyone ever had. Placide recoiled, finally pulling away the mask with force. The void collapsed.

He found himself sitting on a cold concrete sidewalk in front of Duplessi's brick rowhouse in Toussaint Ville with twenty minutes unaccounted for, panting and coated in a sheen of sweat. He pulled himself up and approached the house, still holding onto the mask like a security blanket. Through the window, there was a scene of domestic warmth: Duplessi laughing, Cynthia telling a story, little Denise hugging her father.

Something twisted in Placide's chest. A family. Wholeness. Everything he had lost.

He could knock on the door. They had invited him before. Loved him, in their way. But love, he had learned, was as fragmented as a Loa's power. Conditional. Untrustworthy.

The same reverse cadence that lived in SHIV rose in him—a rejection, a protective mechanism. He wasn't wanted here. Not truly. Not in the way he needed.

He could call Adam, and he almost did, but shook his head. Adam was out running away from his problems in his stupid truck, but that wasn't what Placide did when he was scared or needed answers. Placide didn't avoid things.

Placide stepped back, pulling his mask tight as Papa Samedi's voice croaked at him again. The night swallowed him, his breath synchronizing with the backward song of his soul.

Seed of the Gran Komansman

In the time when Haiti was called Saint-Domingue, Legba saw a pattern among his mysterious family—the Loas. Each rode their horses alone—that is what they called humans. Erzulie's horses reveled in pleasure, Ogun's horses were fortified to withstand punishment, and the Ghede's horses embraced death without fear.

For each human, there was a single Loa riding them. No confusion, no sharing, no union.

Yet Legba sensed a gathering storm on the island. While the plantations enriched a small group of colonists, the enslaved, who vastly outnumbered them, seethed with anger. In Liancourt, Legba approached Anansi, who lounged under a mango tree with his mouth full of fruit. Juice dribbled along his many limbs as he watched a scene unfold beyond the tree's shade.

"Anansi," Legba said, "have you noticed how separate we all are? Each Loa rides a single horse at a time, sometimes a few, but never sharing control amongst us."

Anansi sucked mango fibers from between his teeth. "Isn't that how it should be?" he replied with an exaggerated burp. "I have my horses, you have yours. The humans know who's guiding them—clear lines, no confusion."

Legba gestured out beyond the mango's branches. A slave, once daring enough to flee, now shrieked as he was dragged back to the plantation. His rage and despair bubbled through the air like a poisonous cloud. Anansi swallowed a mango seed, and it stuck in his throat. He coughed, face contorting, limbs twitching. The slave cursed the Loas, cursed Bondye too, wailing until his voice was hoarse. At this, Anansi's cough deepened, as if something unseen gripped his throat.

Legba watched him sputter, eyebrow raised. "Look at you," he said softly. "His anger was enough to choke you just now. These people, these slaves—they don't know how much power they can have over us."

Anansi's eyes bulged, and at last he spat out the seed. It fell to the ground with a wet *plep*. He gasped, glaring at Legba, voice raw. "They can't even unite to kill their masters," he rasped. "There's no way they could even perceive us for longer than a second."

"Not yet," Legba agreed, shrugging. "But these slaves are uniting against their oppressors. We will likely become involved, each in our own selfish way. They will come together temporarily to win their freedom, and at a great, great cost." Legba considered this, casting his mind to the future to consider what might happen. Once satisfied with his calculation, he continued.

"But what if one of them found a way to gather their anger, unite it, shape it into something that could hurt and manipulate us? What if one human, carrying a... seed of fury, joined with others? Their oppressors wouldn't stand a chance, so how would we fare, then?"

Some time passed. Anansi said nothing, still shaken, his limbs trembling slightly as he eyed the slave growing old and bitter. In the distance, thunder rumbled over mountains, echoing the sound of the conch horns blown by the maroons.

"What if we did the same?" Legba said. "If we pooled our influence, guided horses together by sharing their souls, we would form something larger than any single Loa. A structure, or a... company of sorts. More than one rider harnessing one or more horse's power. Many wills forging a single, unified purpose. We could shape a force beyond imagining—become a presence so entwined that no one knows where one ends and the other begins. And they wouldn't know how to hurt us."

Legba stared at the mountains, mumbling with two voices as he sometimes did. "Two into one. It's a contradiction—a crossroads where fates converge. Yet it's precisely at such an intersection that something new can get made. Many riders, one horse. Many souls, one vision. That is the power of unity and *sharing*. Yes!"

With that, Legba turned away, leaving the spider to stew in discomfort. Above them, ripe mango leaves drifted down one by one, layering atop each other like the binding pages of a book that had not yet been written—pages that would one day tell of rebellion, revolution, and the seed that would become the Gran Komansman.

Son of Madame Koupe

Louis Duplessi was glued to the screen of his Soleil PlayKid on the evening his mother lost herself to Erzulie Jewouj. His maman, Veronique, was a short woman with dark brown skin prowling through the aisles of the FabriClose factory. She surveyed the whips—people who had accepted shares of a Loa—while they worked to assemble mechanical Vèvè-Tech shears with salvaged circuitry. Louis sat in his hiding place under a pile of boxes, tapping at the PlayKid's well-worn buttons. He'd hacked his favorite game, *Voyage Fantastique VII*, weeks ago, swapping the default Knight character for a tiny Healer-Louis.

On the dim screen, a turn-based battle indicator slid into view:

PARTY □ LOUIS (HEALER)
ENEMY □ RED EYE (UNKNOWN)
□ SKILLS: CALM • INSPECT • HEAL

Louis chose CALM, and a glowing ring flared around the sprite's feet.

The hovering eye kept advancing. Legba's two-face icon popped into the ALLY slot. The Loa's double-voice came out of the speakers of the purple handheld game system and a deep rumble in the back of Louis's throat.

"She's coming for you," Legba warned. "You may not survive this time."

The screen displayed what parts of his soul had been given to a Loa:

WELCOME TO VÈVÈ-NET!
IT IS 7:45PM IN FABRICLOSE TERRITORY,
PAN-CARIBBEAN AFRICAN UNION.
TOTAL HOLDINGS: 1.54% LEGBA
0.02% DAMBALLAH
0.01% ANANSI

Louis hovered over the option that said "Trade."

"I can protect you from her and give you the information you need!" said Legba.

"Just tell me," Louis hissed, louder than he expected to. Above him, the other whips working on making scissors grew quiet.

A notification flickered:

**TAP-TAP WINDOW OPENS IN 00:12:43
CAUTION — EXPLOITING THIS WINDOW IS
AGAINST THE TERMS OF YOUR AGREEMENT
TO USE THE VÈVÈ-NET! RISK OF LOSING ALL
SHARES IS HIGH.
[LEGBA] — DON'T USE IT. I'M GONNA HAVE
TO REPORT YOU IF YOU GET CAUGHT.**

Louis's breath caught as a metallic ZEKK rang down the factory aisle. Maman stormed into view, her M. Koupe-89 shears raised like a machete. Around her, the other Erzulie whips hunched harder over their work—as if the mere mention of an illegal trading window could slice them in half.

"Tell me when I can do the trade." Her double-voice cracked, half Maman, half Erzulie Jewouj—one of the countless Loas who now interacted in this world by offering shares of themselves to those who were willing to pay. "And don't lie to me."

"I don't know," Louis lied, though he kept his eyes on the ground while trying to scoot back into the corner where he could make himself small.

Maman kicked him once in the thigh, then bent forward and grabbed him by the collar to yank him to his feet. Louis grabbed her wrist and struggled against her, and the PlayKid dropped to the ground. Her scissors were in front of his face now, radiating heat and making his teeth chatter. He felt like a bug about to be fried under a magnifying glass.

"There aren't any more tap-tap windows today!" Louis lied again through a shout, shoving her away as hard as he could. She barely budged, holding those shears aloft and pointed at him. The once-familiar face of Maman was now a distant memory, replaced with a wide-eyed woman who oozed blood from her eye.

Three whips were watching the scene, all wearing white and standing behind their sewing tables.

"Let GO of me!" Louis shouted with a cracking adolescent voice, though his eyes were on the ground. Maman holstered her scissors and released his collar, sending him toppling back. The back of his head hit something hard, and he coughed, hunting for the PlayKid.

Maman, or the woman who had been his maman, turned and stomped away, shouting in Creole at the women who had been watching. The FabriClose workers had not helped him—they just stood watching like stupid statues, all wearing the same white dresses. *I don't give a fuck about any of them,* Louis thought as he booted up the PlayKid and sent his avatar back into the battle against RED EYE. *Maman is gone now; it's only Erzulie Jewouj.*

An updated notification bubbled up on screen:

NEW OFFER: 0.50 OF ⍰ LEGBA: COST: 13 MEMORIES
[LEGBA] THAT'S THE CHEAPEST IT'S GONNA GET. MOVE QUICK-QUICK, TI-LOU!

Louis's thumb trembled... then he hit ACCEPT.

PAYMENT RENDERED: 13 MEMORIES

He wiped away the tears on the screen and got up from the scattered remains of his little refuge in the back of the factory. It dawned on him that he didn't need to hide while using his PlayKid. He could just hold it up as he walked around and navigating the factory would be fine. The bloody red eye of Erzulie Jewouj approached him from multiple angles.

A feeling like cold cement spread through the top of his head to his fingers that clutched the PlayKid. That cement feeling vibrated and pulsed into a slow rhythm, hard enough to rattle his teeth. A new notification popped up next to him. *"Ten minutes left in the Komansman!"*

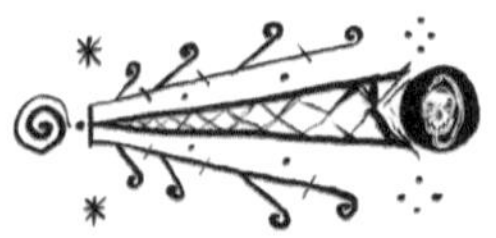

In Louis's memory, that Legba had taken from him as payment, he was at home with Maman, a cramped apartment in Rigaud where she had killed a man the day before with Vèvè-Tech shears. Now, in their kitchen that smelled of garlic and warm butter, Maman stirred diri a pwa in a pot while singing to oldies on the radio.

Louis, sitting on a wicker chair, poked at his PlayKid. The komansman had just ended, and the system displayed his status.

LEGBA HOLDINGS: 0.15%

Maman spoke with unusual cheerfulness, answering his unspoken question.

"Ever since the Bad Sickness took your Tonton Alfred, I swore I'd never let anything hurt us," Maman said, slowing down in her dance as she looked down into the pot of blood red sauce, rendering down. That was why she had killed. It was to protect him, not because Erzulie Jewouj was changing her.

"We used to work like dogs for every gourde, Ti-Lou. Now I just trade pieces of my soul. Pieces of Erzulie Jewouj." She paused, looking down at the pot of bubbling diri a pwa that had cost a fraction of a decimal of a Loa share. "Back when I fixed armored denim for the PCAU enforcers, that was easier." She laughed without humor, eyes drifting to the M. Koupe-89 shears on her hip—once ordinary, now humming Vèvè-Tech since the onboarding.

"Grandma told me Loas used to mount only one person at a time," Louis said, trying to change the subject.

Maman snorted. "That was before the Komansmans, Ti-Lou. Now the Loas work like corporations, and the PCAU's letting Vodouites—people like us—run the show. Even the rich men who owned FabriClose can't boss us around anymore. We can finally take what they owe us and run the factories."

She rapped the spoon on the pot. *Tap-tap.* The double knock made Louis think of those whispered, illegal trading windows on Vèvè-Net.

"How much of Erzulie Jewouj do you have now?" he asked.

She clacked the spoon on the pot rim in time with her answer: "0.9%"

"That's tiny."

"Tiny but useful," she said, covering her left eye to mock her new abilities. "Let me sew faster, and know what to cut." The whites of her eyes hadn't yet started to turn red.

On Louis's screen, his healer-sprite in the game of *Voyage Fantastique* paused before a door marked with Legba's two-faced sigil.

"What if you jumped to 10%?" he pressed.

Veronique laughed, shaking her head as she looked at him. "You play too many games, Ti-Lou. I wouldn't let her have that much of me."

"But what if you tried? Or what if she convinced you?"

Maman held his gaze, smile faltering as she tried to remain serious but light. That was enough of an answer. It was her turn to change the subject as she filled two decorative plates, one for him and one for herself.

"Tande'm... a few of the other seamstresses are heading to the factory. The building is strong, stocked with expensive materials, food, backup generators—good for trading."

Louis thanked her for the food and took a bite. "You wanna live there?"

"Just until it's safe out there," she said. "We can trade shares, watch each other's backs. If a Komansman turns ugly, or those Destructos come hunting, we all have Vève-Tech shears and can make more with all the scrap equipment around."

Louis pictured the factory floor like a cave from *Voyage Fantastique*: mazes, boss battles, but also a place where they could be safe.

"So," Maman said, forcing levity into the mood, "after we eat, you can pack your bags, then we can go in a few hours to join the others. D'accord?"

Louis studied her left eye—still human for now, though that would change during the trip north to the factory.

"D'accord," he agreed, though it was only to make her—and Erzulie Jewouj—happy for the time being.

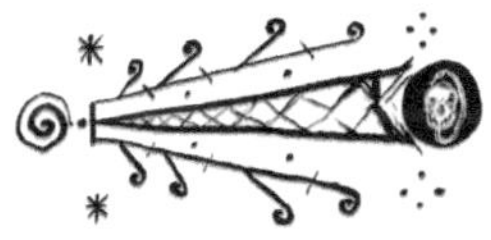

In the next memory that Legba took from him as payment, the Gran Komansman was blooming. Louis crouched on the carpet of Maman's bedroom in their apartment, the door barricaded with a dresser and two chairs. Each tremor outside shivered through the walls like a small earthquake.

They hadn't eaten since yesterday, since they had run out of canned food. Every time Louis tried the radio or the house phone, he got the same thing: a hiss of static that rose into eerie, static laughter and numbers. He clutched Maman tighter as the floorboards heaved beneath them.

Louis had switched his Soleil PlayKid off hours ago to save the last sliver of battery, but now the game system vibrated in his palm and its dead screen flared to life. A flickering pulse filled the screen, matching the shaking all around them.

"The batteries died," he whispered. "How is it even on?"

Rainbow light waved across the bright display, and unfamiliar black text rolled into view:

WELCOME TO VÈVÈ-NET. THIS SOLEIL PLAYKID IS NOW AN OFFICIAL VÈVÈ-TECH DEVICE.
TIME LEFT IN THIS KOMANSMAN: 5 MINS
[LEGBA] —LET'S GET A GOOD LOOK-LOOK AT YOU!
LOUIS DUPLESSI: 14 YEARS OLD, RIGAUD, PAN-CARIBBEAN AFRICAN UNION.
LOUIS DUPLESSI: 61 MEMORY UNITS DETECTED.
[LEGBA] HUH. YOU'RE SMART!

CLAIM STARTER SLICE • 0.11% ⍰ LEGBA • COST 1 MEMORY
[LEGBA]— YOU'RE GONNA THINK I'M BLOWING SMOKE UP YOUR ANUS, BUT THAT'S A GREAT DEAL. I'VE BEEN LOOKING FOR A

WHIP LIKE YOU. YOU HAVE PROMISE. THIS IS CHEAP-CHEAP!

Louis's thumb hovered, then clicked ACCEPT. A hot spark zapped up his arm, the light onscreen flared white, and a deep double-voiced cackle burst from the tiny speakers—reverberating in his own throat like carbonated bubbles. In that flash, he relived the last time his father hugged him goodbye... and felt the recollection sucked out, chopped, and eaten by Legba until only a dull gap was left.

CLAIM SUCCESSFUL: 0.11% OF LEGBA [LEGBA] DON'T MAKE ME REGRET THIS.

Reality and pixels welded together. Map-lines from *Voyage Fantastique* bled across his awareness; Louis could almost see loot-icons hovering over the overturned dresser. Maman lunged, brandishing her M .Koupe-89 shears. The blades sparked, zapping her fingers. "Wooy Bondye!" she yelped at the sensation.

"*Pa geyen problem, Maman,*" the same double-voice purred out of Louis's throat instead of the speaker. "*Take his offer and you'll understand.*"

Maman's eyes flicked to the little screen on the scissor handle. She poked a few frantic inputs, again babbling a prayer. The humming steadied; her grip relaxed as she stared out into the distance.

Maman-ou is a tough one; I'll have to convince her, Legba murmured inside Louis. *She's got a lot more offers on the market than you did. While she's doing that, I recommend you go outside.*

Louis didn't wait. He pushed aside the furniture they had barricaded the door with, hurdling the stacked food tins, dragged the sofa off the door latch, and threw open the front door.

Outside, in the mid-sized city of Rigaud, the world was coated in rainbows of color from the sky. Louis clutched the PlayKid to his chest and looked around with his jaw wide open. Quincy Avenue was cluttered with cars, shopping carts, and bodies. These bodies, he knew, were dead. Some of them convulsed in time with the rainbow above. Louis felt an intense shock in his chest, and his head was overwhelmed with information, as if his eyes were extra big and could take in more light.

A fast chorus of voices came in time with the next thrum of the rainbow sky. "Nou bezwen those Legba shares you got-lot..." Three men in black baseball caps approached from one of the wrecked cars, each holding a plastic shopping bag with something large, bloody, and human-head shaped inside of it.

Legba chimed in. *"Destructos. Corrupt Baron Vit whips. They want your shares of me. Told you it was a good deal. You should run, quick-quick."* Louis ran and mounted the steps two by two until his lungs burned. He tried to get back into his door, but it was locked and he didn't have the key. He hammered on it with a fist. "Maman!"

Downstairs, the men approached, their bloody shopping bags swaying as they chanted again, faster, like an engine made of corpses revving up. "*N-bezwen Legba tout ou-got...*"

The door opened, and Maman stepped out, holding her M. Koupe-89 auto shears in front of her, one of her wide eyes blazing red as she looked out at the Destructos. She snatched Louis by his shoulder and pulled him behind her. The shears, clearly her way of accessing the Vèvè-Net, buzzed with a hum that was both familiar and alien. The simple light that usually indicated the kind of fabric it was configured for flickered, just like his PlayKid had. Was she trading shares at a moment like this?

TIME LEFT IN THIS KOMANSMAN: 23 SECONDS

She pushed Louis into the apartment and tried to shut the door behind them.

The Destructos kicked the door open, teeth grinding in eerie unison. Maman's shears revved, metal screaming.

Louis's PlayKid chimed, throwing up a *Voyage Fantastique* battle screen:

PARTY⍰ LOUIS (HEALER)—MAMAN (KNIGHT)

ENEMY ▯ DESTRUCTOS X3 (UNKNOWN) ▯ SKILLS: CALM · INSPECT · HEAL

Louis chose INSPECT and saw their hands blinking, right above where they gripped the bloody bags.

"Cut the wrist! Make him drop the bag!"

The shears shrieked ZEKK-ZEKK as Maman carved across one of the Destructo's wrists.

The hidden implants within blinked out. The sack thudded to the floor, spraying wires and stolen red Vèvè-Tech matter.

Without his power feed, the Destructo fell back out of the hallway, howling as he clutched his gushing wrist. They fled.

GRAN KOMANSMAN IS OVER. KOMANSMAN CLOSED – ALL TRADES SUSPENDED UNTIL TOMORROW 8:00 A.M.

Twin pound signs flashed, then a concussive double-beat throbbed through Louis's clavicle as though someone drummed there with two knuckles.

Legba explained, *That's an opening, kid. Oya Storm-Hacks are calling it a "Tap-Tap." If you get caught using it to trade, you're gonna get banned from the 'Net or worse.*

Louis looked up from the PlayKid and saw his mother, covered in blood and sporting a bloody nose, blinking hard.

"Look!" He shoved the handheld toward her, desperate to be useful. "The window's gone but... there's something left. Use it!"

Maman breathed in, her eye growing even redder as she was healed, presumably from making a large illegal trade. Legba whistled, as he was privy to something Louis could not see.

"Ti-Lou," she breathed, voice half hers, half Erzulie, "whatever that beat was... do not tell anyone else about it."

Louis clutched his PlayKid and, for a heartbeat, felt the tap-tap echo back: an outlaw rhythm he knew to look out for.

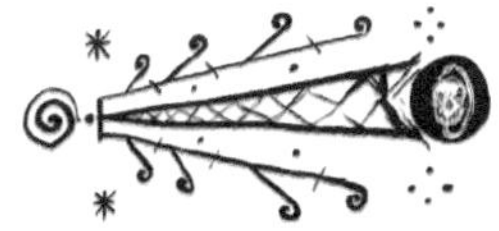

Hours after lying to his not-mother, Louis sat in a corner of the FabriClose factory—PlayKid still welded to his gaze. Only twelve memories flickered in the corner of the notifications, next to a 1.7% LEGBA stake he barely remembered claiming during a frantic tap-tap. The screen seemed to float ahead of him, and when he blinked, the factory floor resolved behind it:

rows of whips collapsed at their machines, Maman, no, Erzulie, crouched at the center, arms swaying. Louis's fingers clenched so hard the purple plastic creaked. A banshee-high wail blurred with the handheld's danger chime. She rose, sweat smelling of bloody copper, and pulled him up off his feet into a frigid embrace.

"Boy," she murmured, voice doubled. "Do you remember what you asked your Maman back in that apartment? She knows what it feels like to get a lot of shares now. I *am* Erzulie Jewouj." Her words vibrated through his chest the way Legba's always did—and something inside them both shifted.

The other whips stayed on the periphery of the room. Maman kept clinging onto Louis, who tried to pry himself away from her cold skin and bloody eye. She was strong, impossibly so. It was like being held by a wall. Behind her, the rest of Erzulie Jewouj's whips were leaving back to their tables to work, as fast as they had come. But it wasn't just that. Erzulie Jewouj was pushing them away. When Maman finally let go of him and went upstairs, Louis picked up the PlayKid and selected his mother's avatar.

Legba spoke with a grim cheer that made Louis recoil. "THAT'S ERZULIE JEWOUJ."

"That's Maman, not Erzulie. I made a mistake. I didn't mean to—"

"TOO LATE. YOUR MAMAN IS GONE."

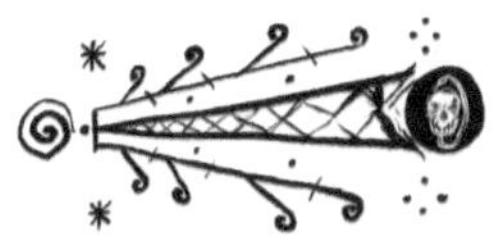

Louis sat on the tile floor of the factory cafeteria, trembling hands gripping the PlayKid on his lap. Maman—or the woman who used to be his maman—sat at a long table surrounded by other workers who waited for her to permit them to start eating their spaghetti dinner. It was Haitian-style, greasy with onions and chunks of fried hot dog. Louis felt his stomach churn, and a hard ball of nervous energy rattled against the inside of his rib cage. He needed to do something, and a part of him was basking in the fact that he had been right. He had *got* her back, dammit. He had told her not to fuck with him, and this is what she got.

Maman raised her M. Koupe-89 shears and jabbed them at the rainbow-colored sky past the windows, close to the ceiling. "Out there, I cannot protect you from Destructos and every other nasty gang who are stealing and killing," she crooned, with a voice that was higher-pitched and slower, like a song. "But here, we are family. They know they can't challenge me. *Ou kompwend?*"

Louis's fingers buzzed with warm lightning as he poked at the purple game console, moving his character in a jittery pattern back and forth in front of two doors at the end of a long hallway. The bright red eye of

Erzulie Jewouj started to crawl up towards him, filling the screen.

"Don't piss Erzulie Jewouj off," Legba whispered, with a new caution. "I've never been strong enough to take her in a fight. Not directly, anyway..." Louis sent his character through the left door and felt the side of his mouth open as he sucked his teeth loudly.

Tchiiiuuup. It went on for three seconds, and Louis could feel Legba cringing as Maman turned and looked at Louis, her left eye bulging now, bright red with blood.

The cafeteria fell silent, and Erzulie Jewouj's whips were looking at him now too. Louis's voice trembled, and inside he felt like he was shrinking, but he spoke anyway.

"It's not just them stealing. We do it too, every time I tell you there's a tap-tap," Louis said, standing up on shaky legs.

"*Ki sa*?!" Maman slashed her scissors downward toward him faster than he could blink, and the motorized blades gave a small ZEKK. Louis stumbled to try and dodge it but slipped and felt the back of his head connect against the ground, hit with a sharp feeling that cut through his thoughts. He bit his tongue, blood coming out of his mouth as he sobbed.

"You're not Erzulie Jewouj! You're my mother, Veronique Duplessi."

The room swam, and Legba was saying things to him, but he couldn't hear. He struggled to get up and find his PlayKid, but Maman was on her feet and holding it, with her other hand pointing her shears at him.

"Give it back!" Louis crawled forward, warm blood spraying out onto his shirt.

Maman's red eye glowed hot, and it rolled independently of her regular eye as she looked down at the game console that contained the only comfort Louis had felt since the world had suddenly come under control of the Loas.

Maman's mouth curled up in a sneer. "I work *ev-wy-day* to make sure those criminals out there don't come in here to hurt us!" Maman said, taking a step towards Louis, and he stepped back away from her, holding up his hands. It's safer now, he shrieked in his mind, the words clogged in his bloody nose and throat. We can go out and survive!

The PlayKid beeped in Maman's grasp, and Legba's voice came out of it, sounding like it was coming through static. "Gimme more memories or she'll KILL us!" Legba whined, and Louis looked from Maman to her scissors to the PlayKid's screen. He knew what was there, even at this distance. The Komansman was almost over for the day, and he had 3 Memories left to give. The screen flashed, and Louis squeezed his bloody teeth together, face growing hot with rage and tears.

"*Ev-wy-day* I have to fight to keep what is mine!" Maman tossed the PlayKid up in the air, and Louis felt his stomach rise up into his throat at the same time. He screamed *no* in slow motion and moved forward, but the woman who was and was not Louis's mother was too fast. Her arms became a blur as she jerked her shears up and down, ZEKKING them twice. Each cut put him in the game, and he was the avatar standing in front of those doors —only he was two Louises, and both wore double-masks like Legba. The nearly empty diamond of memories hanging over his head cracked, and Louis felt his knees turn to hot jelly.

Maman wailed, and the sound was distant but real to Louis as he rolled around on the linoleum floor, unaware of what was down or up. A frantic ZEKK rang in the air, then the wailing multiplied through more voices in the room. Through those multi-wails, Louis heard a split Legba hiss into both of his ears, left and right, up and down, front and behind:

"Remember her—that's all—I can—tell you—"

Louis's vision snapped back into one, and he pushed himself up to his feet on the blood-soaked floor to see his maman swaying in the center of the other whips. She held something in front of her face that was connected by a long string of—no, it couldn't be—

Louis retched. Maman had pulled her left eye out entirely by the optic nerve, the flesh pulsing a mad rainbow like the sky did during the Gran Komansman.

Some of the whips began to break away from the circle and run away as she held her open shears underneath the pulsing bundle of nerves connected to her detached red eyeball.

Maman shouted, to herself—no, to Erzulie. "I will *die* before you take me!" She gestured to cut and then stopped, scissors shaking. Her mouth moved fast, mumbling words Louis could not hear.

"I am Veronique Duplessi!" Maman's voice was one, and her voice was many.

"Yes," Louis agreed, and the part of him that was Legba announced that the Komansman was almost done for the day.

Maman's many voices said: "Don't look, Ti-Lou."

But Louis did look when she shouted, "I am Madame Koupe!" and cut the optic nerve with one great ZEKK.

Maman's body dropped to the ground, and the whips who were left backed away. Louis rushed over to her and pulled her shears out of her hands, gently touching them against his mother's bloody face and the dark, gushing hole where her eye used to be.

Then his memories came back to him. Though his Vèvè-Tech was broken, he could see the game avatars in his mind, and he chose HEAL.

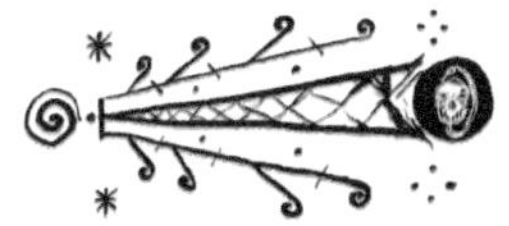

Maman had loved to sing oldies on the radio as she drove him to the school bus stop.

Maman had killed to protect him during the Gran Komansman.

She always danced to Kompa on New Year's, urging him to dance with her.

Maman had wept when the Bad Sickness took Tonton Alfred.

He remembered the bad times, and the good times.

He remembered her name. Veronique Duplessi.

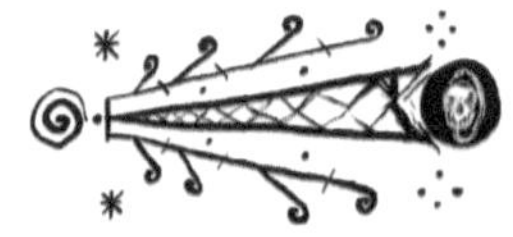

Maman's bloody wound on the side of her face grew bright red. She sat up with a gasp, hunting around with her hands and finding Louis's, coated in some of her blood.

"You're okay, Maman," Louis said, embracing her.

Maman hugged Louis tightly, the way she hadn't done in a long time. He felt that she really saw him, then. "I'm sorry, petit mwen." She sniffled, and he patted her back and shook his head.

"I love you, Maman. It's okay." Louis wanted to tell her he was sorry too—for wanting to give up on her, for hating her so much. He helped clean up what he could while whips—no, the other people—came into the room, looking as dazed as he felt.

"Don't worry," Maman said, embracing those who came forward to check on her. "I think it's time to go outside."

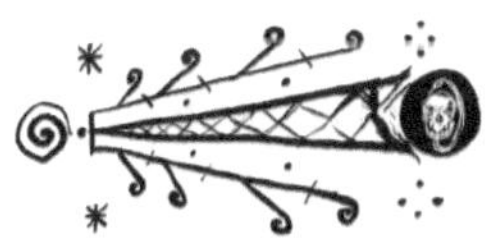

Louis stood beside the factory's large front doors, which had been barricaded by heavy furniture for weeks. He wore a new white jacket and matching jeans. Maman approached in her new white outfit, embroidered with red silk to match her white and red eye patch covering where her left eye had been. He thought the triangular white square on her face made her look like a badass character from *Voyage Fantastique*. Her M. Koupe-89 shears, now cleaned of her blood, rested in a hip holster.

"What do you see?" Maman asked, sounding like herself but with a new steel in her voice that was hard, though not unkind. Her whips were lining up now, all wielding their own shears and packs of supplies.

Louis looked at the door and put a hand on it. The metal felt warm and inviting, like the plastic of his purple PlayKid, now reassembled with sewing equipment and ticking down the time to a new komansman.

"Anansi shares are gonna be on the cheap-cheap." Legba murmured inside of him. "But you'll have to make your way into town."

The PlayKid displayed a window of time on its fractured screen. "You'll be safe out there if Madame Koupe is with you. Shit, I'm scared of her."

Louis turned to look at Maman. "We should go now."

Maman touched the side of his face and looked at him with her good eye—really looked at him. "Merci," she said, imbuing him with a pride in being her son.

Louis looked back at the door and put his hand on the doorknob, which was rumbling with a beat that came from a place he could not see. That beat felt like it contained every possibility—most of them bright and colorful. He bounced his shoulders and took in a deep breath, then turned the doorknob and stepped outside.

Blood Hunt

As Beholders, we have biblical proof that we are the followers and servants of the one true God, Jehovah. All other gods are false, especially Bondye, the so-called 'One We Cannot See,' according to Vodouites.

When asked why we continue to respect the Vodouite-Beholder Treaty of 2002, we answer with scripture: We pay Caesar's things to Caesar, and God's things to God. Caesar may now appear as the relentless, aggressive DTO agent, but it does not matter. We stand rigid in our obedience.

We are legally obligated to abstain from the Vèvè-Net, Komansmans, and other demonic devices of this dying world. But we will always continue to praise Jehovah and proclaim the coming end of this wicked world, as he will soon turn this Earth into L'Après—a blissful paradise free from pain, death, and political corruption!

—BEHOLD! MAGAZINE, DECEMBER 2017

Before Janet's older sister died from refusing a blood transfusion, they had contemplated eternity while preaching the word of Jehovah. They knocked on doors up and down the echoing blue halls of a mega condo in Dessalines, Janet in her wrinkled dress and Josette in her ironed one. Janet started the conversation while they both faced a door that would likely not open.

"Do you ever wonder what L'Après is gonna be like?"

Josette looked down the hallway at the small group of Freres and Soeurs who were preaching with them this afternoon to make sure they were out of earshot.

"We're not supposed to be talking about stuff like this. Especially not in front of..." She pointed one of her well-manicured hands at the door.

"I know," Janet said. "I just *wonder*, you know? Because sometimes it doesn't make sense to me."

Josette pretended to rummage through her purse full of Beholder datachips and *BEHOLD! Magazines*, aware that her younger sister would not let the subject go unless she got an answer. "I think it's gonna be like a giant amusement park world; nothing bad will happen there."

Even in Janet's sixteen-year-old mind, something wasn't adding up. "So, any day now, Jehovah and the angels are going to destroy the world and all of the evil-doers, but the Beholders are going to be safe, right?"

Josette nodded.

Janet gestured, trying to express the world as the shape and size of a bowling ball. "And then, after all those billions of people are dead, the world is going to be made into the big paradise. Pretty pastel colors everywhere, no bad weather, talking animals that won't bite us, all of that." She paused to see if her older sister was still following and in agreement, which she was. Janet continued, leading to her big points, the ones that she really couldn't understand.

"In L'Après, every Beholder who was righteous and died will be brought back to life—"

"The Resurrected," Josette added, keeping her eyes on the stranger's door in front of them.

Janet pressed her hands together. "Yeah, the Resurrected. So, they're gonna come back in waves, but what about all the humans who were righteous but never got a chance to learn about God or the Beholders? Will they be Resurrected, too?"

"Yeah, I think so," Josette replied, though it was without her usual confidence.

Janet tried to imagine the paradise world with all its colors and talking animals and Jehovah looking down on everyone—a great bearded white father with huge suns for eyeballs. "If we and all the Resurrected are gonna be immortal, what are we going to *do* all day? The elders say we'll still have to go to church and stuff, right?"

"That's what they say, yeah. And the Bible, too."

Janet thought that going to church after years of being good sounded stupid. Why would God want them to go to church after they'd already entered L'Après?

"What're you thinking?" Josette asked, pretending to knock on the door again. This would buy them a bit more time before they would have to mark this one as "DID NOT ANSWER" and continue. To do any more might get them in trouble with the DTO. You never knew when they were watching.

"I still have a lot of questions about it."

"Like what?"

Janet turned to face Josette, her eyes unblinking with new focus. "They say no one is going to suffer anymore or die. But they also say that anyone who doesn't accept the truth or is somehow unrighteous in L'Après will be 'Forgotten,' like they never existed. Isn't that like another death, or suffering? How will there be no suffering anymore in L'Après if Jehov—"

Josette hissed, looking over her shoulder again.

"If God is taking you and your memories and trapping you in this eternal world where He can also, like, rip you away from the world and unmake you?"

"Who told you that?" Josette asked.

"I read about it in one of the supplemental materials from the '97 Kingdom Ceremonies Compendium." Janet reached for her personal datapad, but Josette put a hand on her arm.

"You read too much. And you ask too many questions."

Janet felt a twinge of regret at having attempted to ask questions that no one seemed capable of answering. Josette didn't make her feel bad for being curious, but her parents and the Beholders absolutely did. Why couldn't she just be normal and take what was in front of her? Wouldn't that be so much easier? Wanting to smooth things over and pretend like this wasn't at all important, Janet asked a better question. "Remember when Soeur Thompson said, 'We're not going to have genitalia in *L'Après*?'"

Josette barked out a loud, ugly laugh. It was one of Janet's favorite sounds, because it was the only ugly thing about her older sister.

"She was so serious about it, too!" Josette doubled over and held onto the wall, now breaking into belly laughs. Janet almost joined in, but a heavy hand on her shoulder made her shriek in surprise.

"Wouldya like to share what's so funny?" A quick, cheerful voice came from behind them. Janet turned and saw Soeurs Gold and Ravel, two middle-aged Beholder women standing shoulder to shoulder, almost touching hands. Soeur Gold had short, curly blonde hair. Soeur Ravel was bald and wore two small hoop earrings. Her mouth hooked to the right.

Josette recovered from her laugh and straightened. "We were just talking about a cartoon we used to watch."

"A cartoon?" Soeur Ravel repeated, always quick and with a smile. Her eyes surveyed Janet and Josette, lingering more on the older girl, who was almost eighteen.

"Yes," Josette lied, and Janet loved her for it, as her heart pounded and she looked down at her hands, wanting to be away from the older women who always creeped her out.

"We heard what you were asking about L'Après," Soeur Ravel said, and Janet could feel her eyes on her. "The answer to your question is that Jehovah has ways of maintaining purity in L'Après. If He wishes, He can grant Beholders the ability to wipe an evildoer from reality itself." Soeur Gold snapped her fingers to illustrate the speed, and Janet jumped. "Since we're mentoring Josette to train her to Visitor rank, she should have told you this. Isn't that right?"

"Right," Josette said, clearing her throat and smiling through all of it. She was putting on a brave face.

Soeur Ravel blinked at Josette, one too many times. "It's good to see you up and about, and so *healthy too.* Jehovah will reward you tenfold for trusting in him. You don't need those blood transfusions or any of that worldly medicine."

This caught Josette off guard, and her shoulders slumped. Janet looked up then, feeling protective of her older sister who was frequently sick. Soeur Ravel looked back into Janet's eyes, still smiling.

A long time passed, an eternity in silence, and then Soeur Gold spoke, her voice a slow slur. "We've knocked on... all of the doors. Let's... move onto... the next floor."

The older sisters turned and walked away, moving at the same fast pace, lockstep.

Janet let out a breath and shuddered. Josette plucked her ear. "You gotta relax."

"They scare me," Janet whispered as they followed at a much slower pace. "Don't they scare you?"

"They're just lesbians who haven't admitted it to themselves," Josette whispered back, and this sent both of the girls into another laughing fit. The sound of their voices carried down the hallway, where more doors would remain shut until it was time to go home.

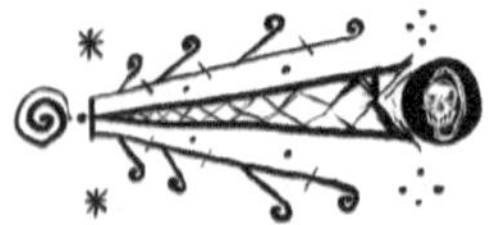

One year later, Josette's condition got worse, and she stayed in a room at Howard City Hospital for testing and treatments. The machines keeping her alive beeped at a steady rhythm, seeming to lead Janet's eyes from the flowers and many gifts and notes Josette got from her visitors. They had come frequently during visiting hours at first, from Beholders to even friends outside of the church. Now, that number had dwindled.

Two doctors came around 11 p.m. to make their final plea to the young girl. Both were light-skinned women, like Josette. Janet watched (or beheld) the scene as if it were happening outside of her body. Witnessing her life from outside her head was easier than acknowledging that her older sister was about to die of something that could be prevented.

"We need you to sign this document on her behalf," said one of the doctors to Janet's parents, who sat by the bedside of the girl who had once been their favorite but was now rapidly losing weight and the life in her eyes. "To confirm her decision to not accept a blood transfusion that could be used as a life-saving treatment for her lymphocytic disorder. This will also release Howard City Hospital from all liability." They handed a datapad to Janet's father, who took it in his calloused, shaky hands.

Papa looked at Josette, then up at his wife, whose expression was blank.

"She decided, *oui*," said Janet's maman, clapping her hands together and looking up through the ceiling at the heavens, at God. "Jehovah's decision. God's decision. Wooy. Please save me. Wooy!" An old-world Haitian grief yelp.

The doctors looked down at their feet and at the window and anywhere else but this ridiculous, murderous family of cultists.

Janet's parents both signed the datapad, and Janet felt a deep sob shake her, rocking her notebook in her hand. How long had she been crying? She pushed herself up from the chair, dumping the notebook on the floor. *Thap.* Then, she shouted as she had never shouted at anyone. "How can you let this happen?!"

Everyone stopped to look at her, and she almost shrank and withered away at the feeling of all those eyes on her, but she kept going. "That's Josette! She's dying right there! No one is here with us! Where are the elders? Where are Soeur Gold and Soeur Ravel?"

Her father used his big, infallible voice on her. "Janet, calm down."

"No, Papa." Janet shook her head. "No. Don't you hear me?"

"I can't believe you twying to make attention to you now," her mother said, her voice softer than her father's. That's what hurt the most. The fact that she was trying to pretend to be rational and calm in this moment. The doctors excused themselves and filed out.

"It's not 'make attention.' How can you say something like that to me?" Janet grabbed the edge of Josette's bed and shook it. Her sister shook with her movements, head lolling to the side of the pillow. "Look at her!"

"Janet." Her father stood up.

"Look at her!"

Her mother slapped her on the face twice, screaming right back, though Janet couldn't understand any of it. A searing pain sparked bright in Janet's ear and jaw. She was on the ground. On the pristine tile floor. The room was so hot, and she was crying.

People were yelling at her. She tried to crawl away, but her father was gripping her right forearm right above the elbow, so hard that she thought it would break.

"Get the fuck off of me!" Janet cried out, wrenching her arm free and not caring if it broke. He let go, and she got her backpack and left the hot room where her whole family was dying.

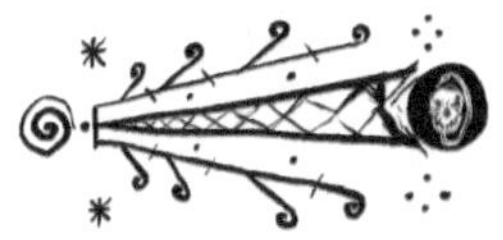

Janet wandered the hospital's sterile hallways, hunting for a way to change everyone's mind. She walked back towards Josette's room, thinking that she could beg her to take the blood transfusion, even though Josette hadn't spoken a word in a week. When Janet was within earshot, she heard a chorus of machines beeping, then a flatline tone, wailing. She ran into the room and then stopped cold, seeing Soeurs Gold and Ravel on either side of Josette's bed.

Soeur Gold held a cylindrical device above Josette's neck with a needle and a thick glass vial on its back, like a metal mosquito. Meanwhile Soeur Ravel read from a physical Bible. Both paused and looked up at Janet.

Janet glanced around the room, mouth agape as she tried to understand what was happening. The flatline continued, piercing the moment. Was Josette dead? Why were her parents and the doctors not around?

Soeur Ravel shouted at her partner. "I thought you took care of this!"

Soeur Gold said nothing, instead focusing on the metal mosquito in her hands as she plunged it into Josette's neck, as if she were doing surgery.

"Let go of her!" Janet charged at the bed, shoving Soeur Gold off. There was a blur, and then Soeur Ravel was in between them, tackling her to the ground and choking her throat. Janet gasped for air, kicking and clawing in vain at Soeur Ravel's arms.. But in that moment, she took in every detail and memorized it. Soeur Ravel's distant look. Soeur Gold's motions as she worked the metal mosquito—the machines around Josette's flatlining as Janet's world faded into a black, dreamlike haze.

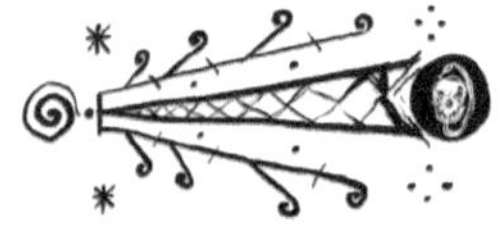

Twelve years later, Janet leaned against a waist-high metro barrier, blending seamlessly into the morning rush of a Komansman. Her gray jacket and chunky sneakers were unremarkable, and her thick, curly hair was pinned into a tidy bun. A passable undercover get-up. Only the subtle twitch of her fingers hinted at the keen focus beneath her calm exterior. Everyone moving past her felt like an open book—every tone of voice, every shift in posture revealing layers of insight.

"Come on, do the facial analysis," Janet murmured.

Anba flickered in disapproval, the Vèvè-Tech glasses pulsing lightly over Janet's eyes. *You've been tailing these two for days,* she whined in Nu-Kreyol. *What are you even looking for?* Only Janet could hear Anba's voice in her mind.

A few yards away, two middle-aged Visitor-rank Beholders stood at the base of an escalator, handing out pamphlets and datachips from a portable magazine rack. They wore DTO-approved name badges—Soeur Vincent and Soeur Floyd—but Janet knew they were disguises.

Anba sucked her nonexistent teeth, dimming her lights in protest. Instead of showing kinesthetic probabilities, she displayed Janet's growing backlog of neglected cases. At the top was one that read "Investigate: Suspected Ghede Vite Whip Evading DTO Officers Repeatedly."

Janet swiped the cases away with a sigh. "I know what I'm doing."

Holding her breath, she watched as Soeur Gold handed a pamphlet to a young girl with a skull tattoo on her face. Anba amplified the voice and sent the data to Janet's display.

"Would you like... a free *bible* study?"

Janet's stomach tightened. She didn't need Anba's facial analysis. These women had changed their appearance in some way, but Janet compared their vocal cadences to her memories. It was them.

Same slow voice, Janet thought, and the words brought a painful cramp to her gut.

Same voice as who? Anba interrupted. *Don't tell me you're following them because they remind you of—*

Soeur Gold and Ravel. She could hear it now in their distinct vocal cadences.

"Shh!" Janet hissed. She refocused as Soeur Ravel gestured towards an approaching Madame Koupe whip in a bright denim combat dress. Janet's eyes locked onto the datachip the older soeur plucked from the back of the rack with unusual care. She handled it with the tips of her fingers as if it were radioactive, or somehow extra holy.

"Ki sa... Told you something was off," Janet whispered.

And I told you to hang back, Anba replied. *We're not close enough to scan legally.*

Janet started walking, checking to make sure her SnapCuffs were properly concealed. "I'm going in."

Don't raise your voice at me! Anba whined.

Janet approached just as Soeur Ravel handed the datachip to the Koupe whip, her voice quick. "If you read this and wanna know more, just call the number." The woman's eyes met Janet's, but there was only recognition in her being a potential mark.

Janet had practiced this moment for years, when she would finally confront the women who'd done *something* to her sister after she died as part of some perverse ritual. She opened her mouth, then closed it.

What's wrong with you? You're never speechless!

The girl with the skull tattoo pelted the two soeurs with loud questions.

"So, you're saying that if we do whatever Jehovah says, we'll get to live forever, but on *this* planet, which is magically gonna get turned into *L'Après*? Is that what you're saying?"

Soeur Gold nodded, passing out more BEHOLD! datachips as a small crowd was gathering, seizing the opportunity to preach. "Yes! Wecanall be a part of the paradise realm!"

The skull-faced girl bounced a datachip along her fingers, making the gold square dance and float. "Oh yeah? All we have to do is give up our lives and refuse modern medicine, right?"

The crowd laughed at this, and Janet was glued to the spot, looking at how this girl was controlling the crowd of people who were simultaneously trading on the Vèvè-Net or on their way to work. She needed to clear them out, but she couldn't break cover. The girl and the two soeurs traded verbal blows as Janet searched the environment for a distraction she could legally exploit.

Trains were coming more frequently into the station, and she was without backup on an unofficial mission. The only exit was a steep escalator that went up several flights.

"Can you make that escalator stop?" Janet asked Anba, who didn't respond. "Please!" Again, no response.

The skull-faced girl was shouting now, getting in Soeur Gold's face. "That's right, bitch. You two killed my sister. Tia Casseus. Remember her?" She thrust out a photo of a young woman who looked to be the same age Josette had been when she died. The soeurs just watched, their placid expressions unchanging. Janet clenched her jaw as a blinding recollection flooded her veins, feeling the hot phantom pain of hands around her neck and seeing the bizarre vision that had come after her sister had died.

This young woman had the same look in her eyes that Janet had when she'd come to in an empty room, gagging and trying to tell her parents what had happened. No one believed her. Her mother still somehow treated Janet like she had caused Josette's death.

Someone in the crowd shrieked. The young tattoo-faced woman was aiming a crude mechanical pistol at the two soeurs, her hand shaking. "I used to be a Beholder, too. That's how I tracked you down here, from your stupid Territory Code system, which was easy to crack, by the way. You *lied* to us! You—"

Soeur Ravel was still the fast one. She chopped her hand down in a blur, and the gun went off with a dull *GLOPP*, dispersing the crowd. Anba flashed red, showing sharp, jagged lines predicting a bad fight. Janet shoved the skull-faced girl aside, sending her sprawling into the magazine stand, and tossed her

SnapCuffs. A satisfying *THUNK* confirmed the girl's wrists were bound.

Before Janet could turn to the Beholders, a fist cracked against her nose. Blood spurted onto her lip and chin, and as she staggered back, thin streams of it floated toward Soeur Gold, who sucked them out of the air and into her mechanical mosquito object, drawn like metal shavings to a magnet.

It's the same device she used to suck out Josette's blood right after she died, Janet thought as she struggled to her feet, horrified. The slower sister jabbed the device into her own arm quickly, her eyes bright with something *wrong*. Soeur Gold went in with a hard kick, and Janet dodged with difficulty, knocking over the magazine rack.

This is fucked! Anba cried out. *DO something!*

They may have been fast, but Janet was stronger than she had been as a girl. She threw an elbow into Soeur Ravel's chest, knocking the woman onto her ass as Soeur Gold swept Janet's legs out from under her. Warning lights blared at her as she fell and rolled over to dodge a series of quick stomps. Then the hands were on her neck again, blazing hot. Something sharp jabbing her arm once, twice. She tore at the powerful hands and threw her elbows back, but the soeur kept squeezing.

"Behold this," the skull-faced girl said, now on her feet and holding her cuffed wrists in front of her. Janet struggled for breath, trying to mouth the word *no*. The skull-faced girl twirled on her toes, head cocked back, and the air in the station sucked into her direction, a hot and shimmering mirage. On the next spin, Soeur Gold flipped in the air too, and only her head connected with the metal part of the escalator with a wet crack. Janet was knocked back onto Soeur Ravel. The older woman let go and crawled to Soeur Gold, crying out and shaking her. The skull-faced girl staggered and sat down, dizzy.

Sirens wailed in the distance. Janet got up and flashed her badge to the growing crowd, coughing as she searched for another pair of cuffs to detain Soeur Ravel with. The woman got up and cried out as she patted down her body, searching for something. She pivoted out of Janet's reach and sprinted onto a train just as the doors closed. Janet lunged and hammered her fist on the door, flashing her badge again and chasing the train as Soeur Ravel glared at her, promising death with those eyes.

"I know you!" Janet wheezed, hammering more as the train sped off.

Are you okay? Anba asked.

"Call HQ. Tell them I've got one body and one suspect in custody." Janet waved away the amateur journalists taking pictures and video. "We need forensics." Anba chirped and called it in.

Janet approached the skull-faced girl, who stared at the Beholder woman in front of her, splayed out in a growing pool of blood. "I'm Special Investigator Janet Baptiste. On behalf of the Department of Treaty Oversight, you're under arrest for murder. What were you trying to do here?" Anba provided the girl's name after a scan.

"Nadya? Nadya Casseus?" Janet asked.

The girl said nothing, just stared at a massive holo-screen playing custom ads.

A bystander pelted Janet with VagabonWare and insults on the 'Net as they shouted, "Fuck Deetoh scum. You're just government lapdogs! The Beholders aren't doing anything!"

Anba took pleasure in lashing out and turning off every bystander's Vèvè-Tech recording capability for ten minutes, causing the crowd to scream and back away.

"I didn't mean to kill her. I mean, I did, but... not like this," Nadya said, barking out a loud, ugly laugh. *Just like Josette,* Janet thought, shaking with the sudden recollection.

Don't do that. You need to focus. The chief is go-ing to want answers, Anba replied with unusual calm. This was serious. Janet had fucked up big this time.

"What were you doing when you were spinning like that?" Janet asked Nadya as the sirens got closer. Nadya opened her mouth, but nothing came out. She was crying, tears rolling down the white skull tattoo that was likely a temporary dermal implant.

Janet wiped her nose on her sleeve, her dark blood painting the fabric. Anba sent a clot to her nose, and she mumbled thanks as she hurried to investigate Soeur Gold's body for any evidence. She found the mechanical mosquito device wedged under the escalator. She pocketed it, silently thanking Anba for deactivating any witness interference.

Lower-ranked DTO patrol officers came down the escalator, moving with clinical efficiency as they covered the body and picked up all the scattered Beholder contraband. The medic tended to Janet's wounds. Janet tried to wave them away, but they insisted, asking her to take off Anba (which she refused to do). As they scanned her and prodded her with stim-sticks, she kept her gaze on the young, tattooed detainee whom she'd seen dance and kill in one motion.

Beyond the arrested suspect, the massive holoscreen swiped through advertisements made just for a twenty-nine-year-old female DTO officer living in the PCAU and recovering from a brutal fight. The screen rolled like an old-school slot machine, then stopped on a bright blue scene of three sleeping humans nestled side-by-side in upright CoffinPods. A cheerful, smooth voice crooned as a glowing hand reached down to pluck their minds out of their heads with care.

"With DieFree, your death doesn't have to be painful," the voice said as the scene faded into a colorful, floral world that instantly reminded Janet of L'Après. In the colorful world, the person who had been resting ran through a field, holding hands with their weeping family. "Trade in 0.4% of your Ghede shares, and we will use a state-of-the-art psycho-replication system to ensure that you get the afterlife you crave. Call DieFree now. It's painless."

Janet narrowed her eyes at this ad, feeling like her mind had been violated, but there was something else that disturbed her. *Is DieFree really painless?* Her brief detour in exploring the thought was interrupted by a sharp, stinging pain in the major vein of her right arm. She winced and yanked her arm back.

"Whoa, *that's* something. Investigator, do you know where this wound came from?"

A red spiral-shaped pinprick on her arm. *One of them stuck me during the fight,* she thought. She shook her head and pulled her jacket back on.

Afterwards, Janet forced herself upright, holding out a hand when they tried to haul Nadya away.

"I'll take her in."

"But this is our patrol—" one of them protested.

"Do you wanna tell Chief why you got in the way of my investigation?" Janet lied, pulling Nadya by the elbow, who had enough sense to stay quiet. The patrol officers continued their cleanup, and Janet yanked the young girl toward the exit.

Not your best work, Anba quipped. *You got a Beholder killed, took evidence, and kidnapped a suspect? You should have listened to me.*

"What the fuck," Nadya sneered at the civilians watching them.

"I just saved your ass. Shut up," Janet replied, summoning her squad car onto the busy street level.

"Nah," Nadya murmured. "I saved yours."

The pain in Janet's arm pulsed as if in agreement.

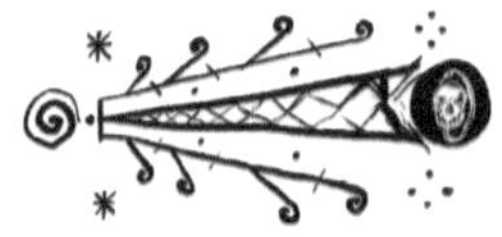

Janet was a shrinking bug under the magnifying glass that was Chief Osborne. He paced around his immaculate, well-lit office, holding his large hands up at either side of his head like he was going to pull his ears off.

"Why do you make my job so difficult?" he asked.

Don't answer that.

Janet cleared her throat. "Because I have the highest clearance rate of any special investigator, ever?"

Chief Osborne lowered his hands and closed his eyes. "I don't give a fuck if you're the inquisitor general. You went behind my back, and a woman *died* on your watch. Then you brought in the murder suspect without following protocol," he said, his voice softer than it ever had been. Janet looked down at her hands, which were clutching either side of the uncomfortable chair she sat in. Her arm, and the odd puncture wound in it, still ached, and it was getting worse. The chief went on. "No more sniffing around Beholder business outside of your caseload. And you know what? No more Beholder cases until you can prove—"

"Chief!" Janet sat forward, and the motion made her arm seize up and spasm. She clutched it and winced.

Chief Osborne went on. "Until you can prove that you know how to stay in your lane. And that little outburst just now cost you an escalation in your caseload. Oh, yes." The man nodded slowly, and Janet kept a hand on her arm, saying nothing.

"There's no Beholder conspiracy that we don't know about. And if there was, I'd make sure to keep you far away from it, just to prove a point." Beside him, his datapad chirped. Chief looked at the screen and poked at something. "The counsel is going to want a full report. Get your arm looked at."

Janet stood, and her knees almost gave out from under her. "Yes, sir," she said.

"You're dismissed."

Janet turned to leave and put her hand on the door.

Don't do it! said Anba. *Whatever you have planned, it's just gonna make things worse!*

"Sir? What's going to happen to the girl? Nadya." Janet knew it was a risk to ask, but this was her only chance.

"She's going to get sent to Valdez," Chief said, and Janet pulled the door open and left just as he called out, "Stay the fuck away from her!"

You're not gonna stay away from her, are you? Anba asked as Janet jogged her way through the fluorescent hallways of DTO central booking.

"Find out how much time I have before she's taken away," Janet said, wincing as she dodged a group of officers.

I can't do that.

"Please! I'll let you watch any shows you want for two weeks."

Three.

"Fine!" Janet skidded to a stop in front of the interrogation room and tried to slow her breathing.

Dummy. I would've done it for one! Let's save that girl.

Janet stood in front of the two officers standing guard—she outranked both. They looked at each other.

"Let me in," she said, dredging up her most authoritative voice.

"You're not authorized, Baptiste," one of them said. "And you're not even in uniform."

"Chief gave me clearance. Now let me in."

They talked among themselves for a moment.

"I've had a really hard fucking day," Janet groaned as she stepped forward. "Do not make me pull rank. Move." They parted. Anba whistled with sincere admiration.

You've got fifteen minutes.

"Fifteen?" Janet almost wheezed as she unlocked the interrogation room with her bioSig. It was getting hard to breathe. She thought she'd have at least two hours. A horrible idea dawned on her. *Someone wants her gone. They're trying to cover something up.* This would mean that the chief wasn't trustworthy. Janet grimaced and dropped her weight into the small metal chair across from where Nadya sat, still cuffed and looking up at the bright lightbulbs.

Anba flickered a notice. She'd deactivated the camera's recording—a temporary and dangerous fix. Janet pulled out the metal mosquito device and held it out to the young woman. "In fifteen minutes, some Enforcers are gonna come in here and take you to Valdez." Her words came out rushed, not how she liked to question anyone. But she pressed on, ignoring how her hand shook. "Do you know what Valdez is?"

Nadya looked down now, eyes wide and lip trembling. That was good. She knew.

"I can help you, but you need to answer my questions honestly. We don't have time." Janet's arm stung her again, and the sharp pain traveled up to her neck.

This isn't right, Anba said. *Your heart rate is dropping. You need a doctor now! Not later.*

Janet shook the metal mosquito device. "Did the soeurs use something like this on your sister?"

Nadya looked away, using her shackled hands to wipe sweat from her forehead. Lips parting, she shook, then murmured, face screwed in contemplation at her options. "I can't. I don't know anything."

Janet tightened her grip on the device. "You may think you know about Valdez, but it's much worse than what you see on the vids. You won't make it a week without having to choose a gang to clique up with. They'll hurt you, and I know you think you can use whatever that secret... thing is that you can do. But they smuggle in Loa shares. I don't know how, but they do it, and whatever you can do, they can do much worse."

The young woman let out a loud, abrupt sob, and it sounded so much like Josette that it made Janet pause, swallowing sour spit. When had her tongue started to taste so bitter?

"You don't know me," Nadya cried out.

"No," Janet agreed, "but you remind me of my sister." She blinked in the bright lights, shocked that she was about to reveal this in her desperation.

"Bravo, is this your good cop routine?" Nadya tried to clap for effect but failed with her hands cuffed.

Janet took a deep breath and pressed on. She was close. Either Nadya would break, or she would. And

Janet knew how to get the information she needed, especially when time was running out and everything was telling her to quit. "Her name was Josette, and she was my older sister. I grew up as a Beholder, just like you." This got Nadya's attention, though she still seemed skeptical. The young woman kept her eyes on Janet as she recounted the short version. About what the soeurs did to Josette, and how no one believed Janet. Not her parents, not the elders. And that was why she had left home and the Beholders.

"I need answers. Just like you," Janet said, her voice lowered to a whisper. "So help me. Please. And I can help you."

Nadya sniffled, struggling to wipe her tears. Janet fumbled a wrinkled tissue out of her pocket and offered it, but Nadya shook her head with an "ew." It made Janet laugh, in spite of the situation, her lightheadedness, and the fact that she only had six minutes left in her plan.

"They did the same thing to Tia. Said they were mentoring her, but shit started getting weird. *She* started getting weird. I think they were using something like that on her," Nadya said, indicating the metallic mosquito device. "She was getting skinnier and weaker, and I had to pin her down to get her to show me her arms." The bright light made her face tattoo stand out more against her dark complexion. She fixed her eyes on Janet's. "She kept saying, 'They can access

L'Après through the blood,' and that the soeurs made her understand."

Wooy Bondye, that's terrifying, Anba chimed in.

Janet stashed the mosquito device, sitting back in the chair, and tried to control her breathing.

Oh, Anba pushed to her mind. *You're doing the Janet Thing again, huh? Well, just remember we don't have a lot of time, so do whatever you're gonna do fast!*

The pieces to the puzzle were there now, and Janet knew it in the way her mind prickled with the possibilities, even in her odd state, and even as her vision began to swim more. But she had to take care of something first. "Thank you," she said, nodding at the young woman. Then she took out a datapad and handed it over, nearly dropping it in her sweaty, shaky grasp. Nadya caught it and looked up at her captor, eyebrows raised.

"There's a—unh—a refugee captive loophole," Janet hissed through her teeth as the pain in her arm got worse.

"Are you okay?" Nadya asked, and Janet held up a hand to silence her.

"You're going to claim self-defense on the soeur who attacked you. And then you're going to join the DTO as a cadet. Name me as your sponsor," Janet stammered.

Nadya shook her head. "Ki *sa?* I'm not gonna join Deetoh; are you *dezod?*"

"You're smart, you have drive but no discipline, and you can clearly use the money." Janet felt pinpricks of her consciousness drifting, as if she were about to fall asleep. "It's this or Valdez, so sign the datapad."

The young woman signed, and Janet thought three words as she slumped out of the chair and hit the ground.

I saved one.

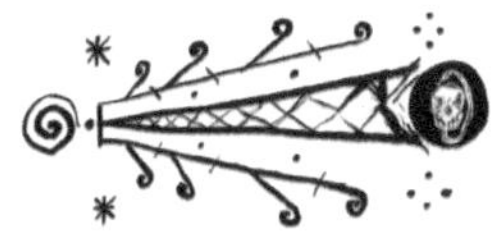

Janet's mind stung with the same pain that had burned in her arm. She thought of the ad she had seen before in the metro, only now the massive screen was her mind, and her awareness was like a camera, shrinking and shrinking into a single droplet of blood on that screen.

It's painless; just ask your sister.

Janet entered the blood droplet, and it flooded her awareness. She was surrounded by blood cells and bacteria and spiky orbs that were viruses. Then, the smell of grass and vibrant happiness. Janet was not Janet in this small place, but something smaller and flatter than a microscope could see. She was a vèvè, a symbol made of lines and circles, and she was a chemical.

"I don't understand," Janet said, but she explored the puzzle pieces in front of her. Somewhere above, people were shouting, and she could hear Anba and Nadya and the two guards who had let her into Nadya's interrogation room. Her body was being moved somewhere for medical attention, and someone was calling her so stupid.

Here, in the drop of blood, she could hear other voices. Too many to count, and they laughed and cheered like the colorful pastel-wearing people in the Beholder literature, and they were being stuck with needles and holding hands together, then they cried and wept blood as the bright, always-sunny world twirled and twirled around them until they became smears. Janet hung onto this idea, this answer, for dear life as her mind blurred.

L'Après was real, and she had the answer to the question she'd asked when she was sixteen.

L'Après was a shared delusion: a prison of minds chained together by blood the Beholders were collecting from their followers, both dead and alive. It was a perfect perversion of their doctrine.

Janet clung to this answer for dear life like a buoy, because knowledge and questions were all she ever had, and that answer took her up and out of this place, back into her body where her journey was just beginning.

RIDING WITH DEATH

The red neon sign of Club L'Étrange pulsed like clockwork, its heartbeat rhythm matching the bass that vibrated the windows of Adam Regis's DeathTruck. He'd reinforced every inch of the vehicle—curseproof glass, hyperclocked twin Anansi Engines, and Ogun Steel where he could afford it. It wasn't the prettiest ride in the city, but it kept his fares alive and undetected by the DTO when things went wrong.

As if on cue, a blood red DTO cruiser rolled by, and the two officers inside turned to glare at him. Word on the street was that they were looking for tap-tap drivers with even more aggressive tactics than before. This was a perfect time to quit the business.

Adam deserved this night off. Baron Vit's shares of his soul were a burning fever under his skin, and a constant reminder of debts he could never shake off. His heads-up display showed the magic number: Baron Vit owned **12.1%** of his soul. Through the windshield, he watched clubgoers drift past, their bodies moving to a frenetic RasinWave beat coming from within. Their excitement, their dancing—it called to him.

He thought in Nu-Kreyol:

Jis yon swa I wanna leave this motherfucker
Jis yon swa I wanna breathe in this motherfucker
Jis yon swa I'mma lage li on the dance floor
Jis yon swa Find a honey ki kone I'm exactly what she asked for
Jis yon swa I don't wanna think about Maman Mwen
Jis yon swa I wanna scream lage'm—

A familiar dry cackle burst from the backseat and right in his ear, shocking him out of his thoughts. His skin prickled and crawled as he felt the phantom touch of two hands creeping over his shoulders. "Fuck off," he grunted, clamping the thought and feeling away. How was he supposed to go and dance in this state? He might not even make it past the bouncers.

Movement flickered in his side mirror, interrupting his brooding thoughts. An older woman in a white-and-red DieFree jumpsuit materialized from the shadows, her hand pressed against his window. The sight of her hit Adam like a physical blow to the throat. She should not be here. She was supposed to be buried in one of those coffin capsules, her soul properly sealed to go wherever she had prepaid for it to go to. Yet here she was.

The dead woman was of a cool brown complexion like his, with worry lines etched deep around big eyes that had seen too much. She could have been his mother's twin if Ednice Regis had lived to see the Gran Komansman—that day of spiritual disruption that rewrote the rules of existence, when the boundaries between living and dead, between human and Loa, had suddenly and violently blurred. When some died and some transformed, and the world discovered that survival was no longer a straight road.

"Help me get to my family," she said, voice muffled through the curseproof glass. Her palm left a faint trace of glowing soul residue dirt on his window. Her voice trembled. "The DieFree people, they're *monsters*. It's not like the commercials."

"No shit." Adam barked out a laugh. "Should have read the fine print."

The dead woman continued, her gray cataract eyes unblinking. "They're coming after me, *now*. If they take me, they'll rip out what little soul I have left and sell it off—turn me into a zombie before I can ever see my family again. I can pay you!"

"With what? You're almost dead." He barked another laugh.

"You can have my soul shares."

"The fuck am I gonna do with a dead woman's shares?"

The dead woman hunted for an answer, mouth quivering. "Please, I know who you are. They say you can drive anywhere."

"Not interested." Adam kept his eyes forward, fingers drumming on the wheel. No dead person could enter or exit his truck. He was safe as long as he stayed where he was. It didn't matter if she'd been dead for two minutes or two years—this was not his problem. The last thing he needed was another entanglement with shares and souls. Baron Vit, a desperate Loa of death's speed, already had too much of him; he could feel it in how his bones ached on cold mornings, in how mirrors sometimes showed jagged white shadows where flesh should be.

"They're coming," she whined, thumping her palm against the window. "Please, petit mwen!"

Who was coming, exactly? Adam glanced at his phone, and it showed the streets behind him. Three vehicles filled with Ghede Nibo whips were coming around the bend—five of them, with dead eyes and rifles, hunting something that should have stayed in its coffin. They were mercs that DieFree hired to track down escapees like this. His phone assessed their speed and lethality, showing a skull. Adam narrowed his eyes, feeling the threat and the challenge. No one was faster or stronger than him.

That's right! Baron Vit laughed from behind Adam, clapping him on the spiky metal shoulders of his leather jacket.

Adam's phone blinked at him, showing a potential cluster of law enforcement up ahead. Their location scrambles were getting better. Of course, this was happening tonight of all nights.

The old woman's form flickered in his mirror: one moment, she was a mostly preserved DieFree customer wrapped tight in her outfit; the next, her body's decay showed through the cracks. A soul caught between life and death, probably after working her whole life and trying to make things easier for her family. Maybe she had been sold as collateral. Maybe someone had scammed her family. Maybe she was part of a DTO sting operation, and he was driving right into the worst night of his life.

Just like before. Just like with Jean-Jacques.

He hadn't picked up the call from his little brother that night, too caught up in his own shit. They hadn't spoken since.

"Fuck it," Adam muttered, unlocking the doors.

"Merci! Woooy, merci Bondye! Merci!"

"Get in the back and be quiet. Please."

The dead woman slid into the backseat as engines roared to life behind them. "My name is Marianne," she called out, patting and rubbing his arms. *Get the fuck off me,* he wanted to say. *You don't know me, and I'm not petit ou. You must be out of your mind.* Adam's phone chimed with an alert. The gang had wheels—medium-tier DeathCars with blacked-out windows and custom plates that read like curse words in Nu-Kreyol. Adam pulled away from the curb smoothly and casually, not wanting to show fear.

His DeathTruck's armored shell caught the first volley of bullets with dull thuds that sounded like distant drumbeats. His heads-up display identified them as Destructos, each whip owing a significant part of their soul to Ogun and Ghede. They meant business. The Club L'Étrange bouncers blasted their horns, urging them to get out of the non-combat zone. Adam was too happy to oblige, rolling out of the immediate area and in the direction of the destination Marianne had given.

"My family," Marianne said, the old woman's voice carrying a mix of hope and guilt that Adam knew too well. "DieFree said I had three months to stay in the coffin-pods. But my grandson's graduation is in four weeks, and my daughter's baby is due in five months, and I—" She swallowed hard. "I couldn't just be locked away while that was happening."

"*That's* what this is about?" Adam shouted and checked his mirrors again. Three vehicles were gaining on him, their headlights hungry. The shares under his skin burned hotter, Baron Vit's whispers growing louder in his head. *Let me have more,* the Loa purred from inside him. *Let me show you why you're my favorite!* He could dump her here, avoid the risk, keep what remained of his soul intact. It would be the smart play.

Instead, Adam stomped on the gas. More bullets were spraying on his truck, one of them almost breaking through the glass. Ahead, he saw the DTO barricade, designed to catch dezod criminals just like him. They weren't going to catch him. Not now, not ever. "Hold on," he said, then drew in a sharp breath and kept his eyes open as he pushed the emergency brake.

Reality fractured like cheap glass as air filled his lungs, and the world became larger around them. Adam gripped the steering wheel tight as they shrank down and slipped into the Vèvè-Net. In the 'Net, white lines of power cut through absolute darkness, forming highways that moved like living things. Adam felt the change begin immediately. His hands gripped the wheel as flesh gave way to bone, decay creeping up his arms like frost on a window. In the rearview mirror, his face was a horror show—half-skull, with eyes burning like he was a cousin to Baron Samedi himself. He could hold his breath for longer and longer each time this happened, but there were consequences.

Marianne gasped, a sound caught between terror and awe. But there was something else in the mirror too—Baron Vit himself, manifesting as a withered ghoul that cackled and clung to Adam's back, smooshed in the space between him and the backseat. The Loa's bony fingers dug into his shoulders like a jockey riding his favorite horse, its yellow teeth bared in a grin that stretched too wide.

"Faster," Baron Vit hissed in his ear. "Show them why you're my favorite whip."

The truck rattled under the force of the pursuit as it tore through the Vèvè-Net's grid. Only one of the Destructos had been able to follow him down here. They were about to overtake him. Too fast. Too close.

Cursed share-heavy shots slammed into the back of the truck, shaking the frame and exploding his back windows. Marianne shrieked in the backseat, her nails digging into the door. Baron Vit was yelling in his ear, loud and raw, barking orders Adam couldn't hear over the sound of his own pulse.

Adam's bony fingers flexed against the wheel. The neon lines of Vèvè-Net twisted and bent—his exit was coming up, but he wouldn't make it in time. He was starting to lose consciousness. He would have to take a breath.

Turn left! NOW! Baron Vit snarled. *Get past the Deetoh barricade!*

"Go straight!" Marianne screamed.

Adam slammed the brakes. Hard.

Jerking the wheel, he twisted—not in the direction of the exit, not anywhere that made sense. Just away. Away from the Destructos, away from the bullets, away from the snarling weight of Baron Vit in his skull.

The moment his tires skidded across the glowing lanes of Vèvè-Net, something cracked open.

The road vanished, and gravity flipped.

They burst out on a rolling slope of emerald grass, bright as springtime from a dream. Towering, pastel-hued mountains rimmed the horizon, their peaks sprinkled with powdery snow. The sky overhead was a crisp, unbroken blue, and swaying wildflowers blanketed the meadow. Adam's DeathTruck jolted and slammed onto the soft turf, lurching into a sideways slide before regaining traction.

L'Après.

Adam's breath caught. Baron Vit's cackling presence abruptly vanished from his head, leaving a silence that was almost too loud. It was as if a chain had been lifted from his mind, the Loa forcibly barred from this place of unnatural calm. Marianne let out a gasping whimper, fingers clutched tight around her seat.

Small clusters of Beholders were scattered across the meadows, strolling hand in hand like docile tourists.

They wore neat, lightweight clothes in subdued, earthy hues, pressed khakis, crisp linen shirts, and flowing spring dresses. Their expressions were blissful, almost vacant. A few turned to watch the truck skid through the lush grass, but their faces showed no alarm or hostility, just a dull curiosity that felt as alien as the landscape itself.

Adam wrestled the wheel, fighting to keep control as the truck rolled downhill, crushing wildflowers under its tires. Every rotation sent dirt and grass clods flying. He couldn't catch his breath: The air felt too pure, too thin for mortal lungs, and his heart pounded with a dizzy mix of awe and panic.

Maman could be here, flashed across his thoughts, as much a hope as a terror.

Marianne's voice trembled. "Adam..."

Among the calmly watching Beholders, one figure stood out—a woman in a black DTO coat who was stumbling through the field and clutching onto her arm. She looked as though she were searching for something, and stuck in that searching, her eyes snapping and rolling at impossible speeds. Her eyes flicked up to Adam's rampaging vehicle with a warm, frantic plea to help her where she was going. She didn't belong here either, but she was dangerous, and his heart ached to be closer to her in any way possible, because he needed to take her anywhere she desired if he was with her.

Adam panicked and stomped on the gas, despite his desire to stay. The engine screamed, tearing muddy ruts through the meadow. The world splintered under the truck's frantic momentum, and the scenery erupted into streaks of color, as though the entire dreamscape were being ripped away in strips.

In a heartbeat, the Vèvè-Net snapped them back, and the world shrank around them. The neon-lined roads swallowed them whole again. The Destructos were gone. Marianne was panting, her hands shaking. The truck was silent.

Except for the voice in Adam's head.

What the fuck was that?

Baron Vit's voice was hoarse. Not laughing. Not taunting. Just raw, furious confusion.

Adam flexed his hands over the wheel, staring at them. They felt wrong. They felt like they hadn't been attached to him for a second.

"I don't know," Adam said.

Baron Vit exhaled, a slow, deliberate rasp.

You went into L'Après and came out? You shouldn't have been able to do that!

Something crawled up Adam's spine.

When they'd burst back into reality, they were far on the other side of DTO's barricade. Adam let out a breath and hammered his cold, clammy fists on the dashboard, bellowing in triumph. Marianne pointed ahead. Her neighborhood stretched peacefully before them. Rowhomes with warm windows, couples walking together, the kind of quiet that felt earned rather than empty. No pursuers. No sirens. Just streetlights and her small family standing outside of her house, all wearing white—it was a Vodouite wake for her.

Adam's flesh had returned, but he could still feel phantom bone beneath, still taste grave dirt in his mouth. His shares throbbed, higher than ever. Each dip into Vèvè-Net left him a little less human, a little hollower. And this time, he had gone farther than he ever had before.

"I can transfer my Legba and Maman Melanj shares to you," the woman said, reaching for him with hands that should have been in L'Après somewhere. "You risked so much for me—"

"Keep them." Adam's voice was gravelly and sharp. "Stay with your family. Make it count."

She wailed one last time, then slipped out of the truck. Through his window, Adam watched her hurry towards the family. Voices called her name— "Maman!" and "Grandman!"—with joy and relief that made his chest ache. Some shouted, complaining that she had even come back or asking what they would do now. A little girl ran out to hug her, and for a moment, the woman's form stabilized, all signs of decay vanishing in the face of such pure love.

Adam pulled away before she could look back, before she could see what that rescue really cost him. His reflection in the rearview showed normal flesh, but Adam knew better. Each time he called on Baron Vit's power, the decay lingered longer, dug deeper. Baron Vit now owned 14% of his soul. One day, he might look in the mirror and find a skeleton's face staring back.

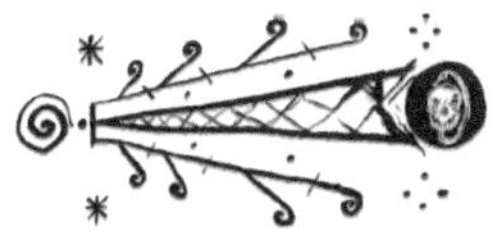

The Club L'Étrange sign still buzzed in the distance, promising forgetfulness in substances and beats. Adam turned toward it, hoping the music might drown out Baron Vit's anxious laughter, still echoing in his skull. One night of forgetting. That's all he needed.

But as he drove, he couldn't help checking his mirror, watching for others who might need one last ride. Maybe that's what Baron Vit saw in him—not just another soul to claim, but a driver who couldn't help but stop, who'd risk his own humanity to preserve someone else's. And there was something else. He thought about that woman he had seen in *L'Après*, with the eyes hunting and seeing everything, every possibility, including him. Had she been real?

The bass from the club grew louder as he approached, but it couldn't quite drown out the whispers. *You're mine now,* Baron Vit seemed to say. *But at least you make it enjoyable.*

Adam parked his truck and stepped out into the night, feeling the phantom weight of the Loa still riding his shoulders. The club beckoned, promising hours where he could pretend to be just another face in the crowd. But he knew better now. He'd always be the man who stopped, who helped, who paid the price—and somehow, that felt more like victory than surrender. Despite everything, he couldn't help but bounce his way into the crowd.

Afterword

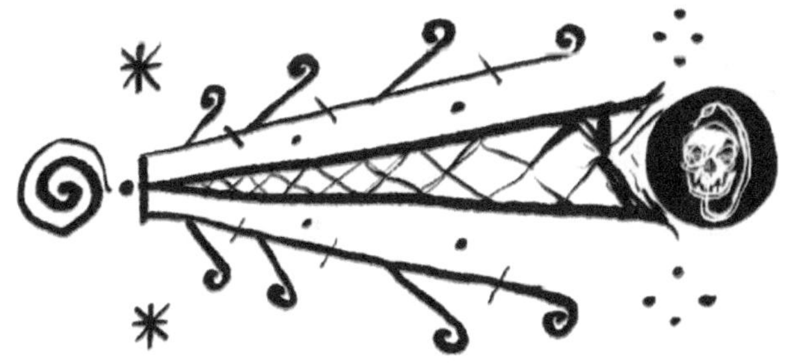

This book, and the ideas and characters and stories in it, came in varying speeds and sizes. Some just showed up fully cooked and ready to go. Others had multiple forms, requiring me to write and rewrite and then wait years before rewriting again. It was not easy, but it was—and still is—a life-affirming feeling to be with you in this space and to say, "here's what I think about all this whole being a human thing. This is what it's been like for me." I'd like to tell you a few things about each story and how they formed.

Ednice and the Gardener

This story had a powerful, explosive origin. I wrote "The Ongoing Revelation of Ednice Regis" maybe a year prior. The problem with "Ongoing Revelation" is that you miss a lot of context if you read it alone. If you're feeling adventurous, go ahead and try reading it without "Ednice and the Gardener" to explain things about the world. How did Ednice learn about the myth she tells the reader/listener about? What kind of world is she in? What are we to make of this myth that she's imparting to us? One of my editors graciously pointed these questions out to me, and although I balked at the advice to start, I considered it and the advice was right.

I have been secretly shipping Ednice and Bondye for the longest time and thought that I was going to reveal this in a future story, but when I tried to answer my editor's questions, this story came out. I knew that Bondye loved Ednice and she loved Him. I knew that they were both trapped, in their own way. And I knew that Ednice's ability to talk and teach was a cosmic level weapon.

When all of this happened, I was on a long stretch of time away from my day job that allowed me to think hard about Ednice and Bondye. I saw her running through the beautiful, terrifying fields of L'Après wearing her hat, running away from her lover who had lied to her. I wrote the first draft of this story over three days (which is rare for me). On one of those days, I woke up at five A.M. with full energy, and I wrote for maybe five hours (that's also rare for me). Like I said, it was explosive and just came out, and I hope the story reflects that energy, because it's one of my favorites.

The Ongoing Revelation of Ednice Regis

My mother (who I dedicated this book to) was a powerful teacher and lover of knowledge. Around the time she found out she was sick with what Haitians used to call "the Bad Sickness." She dove deeper into the Jehovah's Witness doctrine that she had been casually studying at the time. She became what the Witnesses call a "pioneer," which meant that she spent a LOT of time preaching. She would take my brother and I out to knock on doors, and I remember doing so very early on, around four years old.

When I was imagining Ednice Regis, a Beholder Soeur who was dying, I wondered what would happen if she died, went to L'Après as promised, but then realized that the afterlife wasn't what it was cracked up to be. And what if she started to get prophecies revealed to her just like the all-stars of the Old and New Testament? I wanted to try and mimic the texture and style of the Bible verses and passages I read and recited countless times as a kid in church.

The Birth of the Loas

Continuing my desire to mimic the creation stories of the Old Testament, I thought about ways of replacing what I learned with a new story—one centering Bondye. Inside of this one, I tried to describe my intent for the whole narrative arc of what I want to make with the world of Vèvè-Punk.

The First Bride of Erzulie

There are countless stories and ways in which we can (and likely have) encountered Loas in this life, and in this story, I wanted to establish the basic means of interacting with Loas in the days before the Gran Komansman, or even what we call the "Common Era".

Gens de Couleur

In this story, I'm introducing you to what happened in my version of 18th-century Saint-Domingue (now Haiti). This is hopefully going to set the stage for the PCAU, or the Pan-Caribbean African Union, that eventually becomes a world superpower by about 1940. Fabienne Casseus is based on Minette, a real singer from Saint-Domingue who was the protagonist of Marie Vieux-Chauvet's *Dance on the Volcano*. Fabienne is also the main character of my upcoming point-and-click video game, *Vèvè-Punk: Mind Singer*, which is in the R&D phase. You can learn more at <u>domrabrun.com/mindsinger</u>.

This story was a great way for me to use one of my favorite bizarre historical facts. The French had many combinations of "racial classifications" in Saint-Domingue, sort of like Pokémon. There is something so diabolically French about declaring that someone isn't merely colored or black, but "griffe" or "metif." One last thing about Fabienne, with a little bit of a spoiler alert: She and Ti Blag are the direct ascendants of Nadya Casseus, who shows up in the story "Blood Hunt."

Grief in Reverse

How does absolute power corrupt? What would cause you to stand up and say, "I can fix what's going on in Haiti! I have a plan: Listen to me and only me!" Dr. Jean-Jacques Placide is my selfish, bizarro-world answer to that big, multifaceted question. I have a deep, soft spot for Dr. Placide, which is what I hope will make him a compelling antagonist. There's a part of me that will not accept how things are and wants everyone else to reject reality, too. He is my way of exploring what that might be like, the consequences be damned. And those consequences will get much worse for everyone in future stories.

Seed of the Gran Komansman

Loas are fun to write, Anansi especially. It was not fun to write about him and Legba watching suffering happen and doing nothing, but I feel like this mirrors the ways in which we hear and witness horrible atrocities today. To do anything but run out in the street and scream with cardboard signs above our heads makes me feel like we're all Anansi under that tree.

Son of Madame Koupe

Another strong, long story. This one took a lot of different forms and a couple of years and multiple iterations. Louis Duplessi started out as an Adam (in true Vodou fashion), then eventually splintered off into a bunch of other Adams and settled into the form you read him as. Louis Duplessi became a way for me to de-

scribe one of the ways in which the Gran Komansman
took effect.

Blood Hunt

Back when I was a Jehovah's Witness, I spent a
considerable amount of my childhood and adolescence
feeling sad and trapped. I was trapped in the doctrine
that alienated me from my body and mind and history.
I was trapped in churches, auditoriums, and people's
front porches where I did not want to be knocking on
their doors. For many of those years, I was plagued
with a miserable feeling like I would never get out of
the religion, and I would get old with a wife and kids
that I hated and survive Armageddon and then—if I
were lucky—I would live forever in a "paradise Earth"
surrounded by immortal Jehovah's Witnesses who did
nothing but go to church and eat vegetables all day.

Janet Baptiste showed up a little bit after Adam did,
and she had a background like mine, except it was
worse and a lot more dramatic (which is bad for her and
good for us). If you happen to be trapped in a situation
like I was, I am telling you that you can and should
talk to someone trustworthy and impartial about how
you're feeling. I can attest to the fact that life is so much
better on the other side. I wouldn't be here sending my
words to you if I had stayed.

Riding With Death

Back during COVID when I was quarantining at
home and felt like I was going nuts, I decided to finally

start finishing what I write. Adam is one of the first characters that came to me back then. Much like a Loa, he has taken many forms and many names. But the constant is that he always sounds and looks the same, and he always drives. He is a man of few words, and I think he's probably uncomfortable about me telling you all his business. The title of this story is from my favorite Basquiat painting.

GLOSSARY

Adam Regis – A driven Vodouite man obsessed with speed and danger. He is a prominent whip of Baron Vit, the Loa of death's speed. He transports living and dead cargo in his custom DeathTruck, but his main way of making a living is through Tap-Taps—illegal Vèvè-Net transactions outside of legal Komansman hours.

Anansi – A storytelling family of Loas. A lot of people think that Anansi is all about tricking you to do stuff, but it's deeper than that. Anansi is a weaver of realities and unrealities. Anansi whips tend to be creative and concerned with power—especially their own.

Anba – That's me! I am a zemi. Old-school immortal spirit-sculpture from Ayiti. Right now, I'm a pair of telepathic glasses sitting on Janet Baptiste's face. I'm not gonna tell you how we met because it's a long story.

The Bad Sickness – A widescale acquired immunodeficiency syndrome caused by strains of SHIV (**Same-**

di-Immunodeficiency Virus). It killed millions from the 1970s through the late 1990s.

Beholder-Vodouite Treaty – A technology and trade between the Vodouites and Beholders to prevent war. Mainly, it gives the DTO the power to make sure neither side is stepping on the other's collective toes.

Beholders – Jehovah's devotees. They started as a protestant Christian organization and grew to become the second largest political faction on the planet, behind the Vodouites. They are up to something weird with some illegal blood-related Vèvè-Tech.

Bondye – Our supreme creator of everythingness and nothingness. Bondye is impossible to understand, so you may as well not try too hard. That's why you get to interact with zemis and spirits and loas instead—we're like an interpretative buffer. Right now, Bondye is in kind of a rough spot, and hasn't even communicated with us in a while.

Chaquepana – A healing family of Loas. Chaquepana is the head honcho of everything medical and is behind every virus and illness, including the Bad Sickness. Chaquepana whips tend to be involved in the medical field and have extraordinary abilities to interact with biology.

Coffin-pod – DieFree's major technological offering. Upright coffin-sized devices that sustain dying bodies while the mind constructs its own simulated paradise. The system was marketed as universal, able to accommodate any belief system, and it quickly grew in popularity as a cheaper alternative to burial or cremation. Families can even "chat" with their deceased loved ones through external screens linked to the pod. There are rumors that Coffin-pods don't work as advertised. It's creepy as fuck, if you ask me.

Daasi – A Vodouite woman and one of the first Erzulie horses.

Department of Treaty Oversight (DTO) – The DTO is the neutral enforcer of the Beholder-Vodouite Treaty, preventing all-out war between Vodouites and Beholders. DTO agents are former Vodouites, Beholders, and every faction in between. They investigate and prosecute any level of breach in the treaty. They're not supposed to have any access to the Vèvè-Net as part of their impartiality. Between you and me, they're not neutral, even though they're supposed to be. Colloquially known as "Deetoh."

Dezod – Nu-Kreyol slang. It means "bad in a mischievous way."

DieFree – A company founded by a conglomerate or "nation" of Ghede loas. DieFree promises the dying a tailor-made afterlife. They are currently the largest company in the death industry and employ dubious methods of extracting shares from their customers. DieFree is always on the news because of some scandal. I'd advise you to avoid them. What's so bad about dying the old-fashioned way?

Ednice Regis – Ednice is a deceased Beholder-turned-Vodouite who is currently in L'Après. This technically makes her kinda mostly dead. She was once misled by the Beholder doctrine and is now trying to dismantle Jehovah's tyranny from beyond the grave. Best of luck to her. She was the mother of Adam Regis and Dr. Jean-Jacques Placide. She's known to be a complex, intelligent teacher and speaker. The Beholders are not a big fan.

Erzulie – A family of Loas concerned with love, sensation, and creation of all kinds. If that sounds kind of vague and all-encompassing, that's because it is. Erzulie can and does end up in many places. Erzulie whips tend to be passionate, sensitive, and adaptive.

Fabienne – A talented singer who lived in Saint-Domingue. If you haven't heard of her before, you've been living under a rock. She became a freedom fighter and was instrumental in kicking off the events that helped the PCAU (then known as Haiti) become a world power.

Ghede – The family of Loas governing death. This includes the death of intangible and inanimate, abstract things. They're blunt, crudely humorous, and sometimes creepy. Ghede whips tend to be intensely conscious of their mortality and embrace mystery.

Ghede Vit – The Loa of death's speed. He witnesses and encourages the deaths of things. People, ideas, cities. He tends to present himself as a thin man in a black suit and loves a challenge. Adam Regis is his top whip, though he won't easily admit it.

Gran Komansman – This is that big day in 2002 when Legba finally convinced most of the Loas into joining the Vèvè-Net, a techno-spiritual stock exchange that allows them to share portions of themselves fractionally.

Horse – An old word that Loas used to describe humans that they would "mount" or inhabit temporarily, usually one at a time.

Janet Baptiste – My partner, and my best (human) buddy. She's an intelligent, inquisitive ex-Beholder turned DTO special investigator. She cannot get over the death of her older sister, Josette, who refused a blood transfusion when she was a teenager.

Dr. Jean-Jacques Placide – An intelligent, reserved doctor who is developing novel techniques to diagnose and cure diseases. He's being mentored by Dr. Louis Duplessi and is a prominent whip of Chaquepana.

Jehovah – A shard of Bondye, rebellious and arrogant. He sprouted out of Bondye and had the nerve to think that HE should be the one in charge! Obsessed with order, Jehovah imprisoned Bondye within the gem of creation. He's the leader of the Beholders and is really obsessed with blood. You can think of Him as the universe's greatest vampire.

Komansman – Daily, time-bound windows when humans and Loas can trade fractions legally on the Vèvè-Net.

L'Après –A realm of the afterlife where many humans go after they die in this world. Jehovah may have created it, but the Beholders aren't the only ones inhabiting it. It's all vibrant colors and smiling people, just like on the Beholder brochures. That's all I'm gonna say.

Legba – A family of Loas oriented towards openings, gates, and crossroads. One of the heads of the Loas. He was the main one to come up with the ideas of what became the Gran Komansman and Vèvè-Net. You can't even access the Vèvè-Net without getting a small Legba share. Lega whips tend to be analytical leaders.

Loa (Plural: Loas) – To call them spirits is simple, but that's the word I'll use to describe them. They exist between you, humans, and Bondye, embodying every aspect of reality. They are like us in many ways—they have desires, likes, and dislikes. Most Loas are multiple and exist as "families," with different sides and names. Loas used to tend to mount humans (or "horses") one or a few at a time, and temporarily. Legba convinced most of the Loas to band together and split themselves, to be shared and fractionally mounted by humans for longer periods of time—that was the Gran Komansman. Now, Loas are traded by Vodouites daily during Komansmans on the Vèvè-Net.

Louis Duplessi – A smart, curious boy who always has his nose stuck in his Soleil PlayKid handheld gaming system. His mother is Veronique Duplessi.

Madame Koupe – There are rare occasions where extraordinary humans can become Loas or at least transformed to something close to that level. Madame Koupe is one of those occasions. Madame Koupe whips or followers tend to be focused on justice and creating the most fabulous clothing on the planet. I'd wear their clothing if I had a body.

Nadya Casseus – An inquisitive teenage girl seeking revenge for the death of her sister. She has a white skull tattooed on her face, and a mysterious innate ability. Janet sponsored her to enter the DTO academy. Let's see how it turns out for her.

Ogun – A family of Loas who embody strength, battles (internal and external), and steel. Ogun whips tend to be warriors and military officers of every kind.

Pierre-Richard "Papa Samedi" Samuel – A doctor who cured diseases in Haiti, became a dictator, and then unleashed The Bad Sickness when he started to lose power. It's best not to talk too much about him right now, or ever.

The PCAU (Pan-Caribbean African Union) – A world superpower led by Haiti. Controls the Vèvè-Net. Includes the Caribbean, portions of North America, most of Africa, South America, and Central America.

SHIV (Samedi-Immunodeficiency Virus) – Papa Samedi created the virus. It causes what was known as "The Bad Sickness," which ravaged the PCAU from the 1970s through the 1990s, claiming millions of lives, including Ednice Regis.

Soeur Gold – A Beholder Sister from Janet's past. Slow-paced with slurred speech patterns. Generally untrustworthy and scary.

Soeur Ravel – A Beholder Sister from Janet's past. Fast-paced with quick speech patterns. I think Janet should stay away from her, but when does she ever listen to me?

Soleil PlayKid – A purple handheld gaming device. A favorite toy of Louis Duplessi that became a lot more as time went on. He's practically fused with that thing.

Vèvè – The sacred symbols humans used to draw on the ground to summon Loas- traditionally with cornmeal. Vèvès are really complicated and hard to put in one category. They're kind of like cosmic homing beacons mixed with calling cards between dimensions. They are the backbone of how information is shared and transferred behind the scenes.

Vèvè-Net – A techno-spiritual stock exchange linking Loas and humans (also referred to as "whips"). Through it, Loas trade fractional shares of their energy, while humans offer fragments of autonomy, memory, or willpower in return. Each transaction strengthens or diminishes both sides, binding them in a volatile economy that shifts daily during Komansmans, the sanctioned windows when trading between worlds is legally permitted.

Vèvè-Tech – Assorted technologies infused with vèvès. These allow Vodouites (and sometimes sneaky non-Vodouites) to access and interact with the Vèvè-Net and Loas. I've got some Vèvè-Tech going through me, which is why I can exist as a pair of glasses on Janet's face! Vèvè-Tech comes in all shapes, sizes, and forms. Do not underestimate a piece of Vèvè-Net just because it may not look impressive.

Tap-Tap – Komansmans are the legal windows when you can trade shares on the Vèvè-Net, but there are illegal windows where you can trade. These are called Tap-Taps as an ode to the transportation industry in Haiti, and because of the original call sign for the Vèvè-Net back in the day. Every Vèvè-Tech terminal flashed a double-pound sign on repeat, and everyone felt the two taps. Smart and sneaky users took advantage of this. Now, law enforcement organizations can monitor and request patches on Tap-Taps. If you get caught using them, the punishments are severe.

Whip – You humans prefer to call yourselves this when you're mounted by a Loa. Inspired by street-talk, it's the new way to say "horse." I'm sure the term will change at some point in the future.

Vodou – Some call it a syncretic religion, some call it a science of the spirit, or a way of perceiving reality.

They are all right. Vodou was created by Bondye as a "way," and was adopted by your Taino, West African, and Caribbean ancestors. Vodou is a mystery filled with questions and contradictions, and is the system that drives the Vodouites, the most powerful faction on the planet.

Vodouite – Humans who have any level of access to the Vèvè-Net. Most Vodouites live in the PCAU, but not all PCAU citizens are Vodouites.

Zemi – That's what I am! A Zemi is an old-school stone immortal spirit-sculpture from Ayiti. Are we objects or spirits? The only proper answer is "yes."

Acknowledgments

Here it is, the part of most books that I glance over, thinking, "Oh, that's nice—oh, I know that person, and I don't know many of them." Bear with me for a second here. Many people helped me to get here. Leslye Penelope; Alex Jennings; Edwidge Danticat; 'Pemi Aguda; dave ring; my editors, Olivia; Sydnee; Cameron. Thank you to the many writers who I have met and continue to commiserate with through my amazing writer's group and conventions. Lisa Osborne, and the Mind Singer development team continue to help me make my video game dreams come true.

To my family. Dave; Matante Erla; Matante Marie; Kenny. The story of what you have meant to me in this reality would have had fewer battles and a lot less drama. But thank you all.

I want to thank the Washington Project for the Arts for funding this kind of project. As well as Maryland State Arts Council and Black Public Media.

Thank *you* for being here and for reading this far.

RECOMMENDED READING

The Black Jacobins, by C.L.R. James – This is a seminal, accessible text that will give you an overview of the Haitian Revolution. After reading this, refer to it whenever you get a whiff of the racism and ignorance surrounding the events and actions taken by Haitians to win their freedom. It is critical for us to understand what happened for us to link it back to what is still happening. This book will help instill pride in this history, no matter what people have to say about it. Anyone who claims to be lovers of freedom should know and praise the story of Haiti's history, and this book is a champion of that.

The Drum and the Hoe, by Harold Courlander – A great anthropological text describing many aspects of spiritual and musical culture in Haiti.

Flash of the Spirit, by Robert Farris Thompson – One of Jean-Michel Basquiat's favorite books, and one of mine. Thompson digs deep into African and African diasporic art. He carefully and respectfully describes the spirit, function, and design of African and Afro-Caribbean art. I think this book is like the art history equivalent to what C.L.R. James was doing in *The Black Jacobins.*

The Uses of Haiti, by Dr. Paul Farmer (with a foreword by Noam Chomsky) – For you politically scientific minds out there, I recommend this book. Dr. Farmer was doing incredible work globally to help treat and prevent HIV and AIDS and had an expansive point of view on the "why" of it all. He theorizes a few geopolitical "reasons" why Haiti may be in the political situation it is today. It was written in the 90s so it ends optimistically during the Aristide presidency, but I think it's worth checking out. I don't believe in trigger warnings, but I will say that this book is not for the faint of heart.

The Haiti Reader, edited by Laurent Dubois, Kaiama L. Glover, Nadève Ménard, Millery Polyné, and Chantalle F. Verna – A treasure trove of non-fiction and fiction texts all about Haiti, going back to the 17th century to now. This book introduced me to zemis.

Krik? Krak! by Edwidge Danticat – Edwidge's connected short story collection is brilliant, haunting, and potent. It contains a world.

Brother, I'm Dying, by Edwidge Danticat – Brutal and heartfelt memoir that brings dignity to Haitians and the many Haitians who have left the country for a better life only to find something much worse.

Dance on the Volcano, by Marie Vieux-Chauvet – This novel partially inspired my story, *Gens de Couleur.* Follow the tale of Minette and be sure to stick to the last 10% of the book, because it gets totally insane in a great way.

Tell My Horse: Voodoo and Life in Haiti and Jamaica, by Zora Neale Hurston – Zora told a story of a very particular, singular Haiti, but I think it's still quite valuable.

Hadriana In All My Dreams, by René Depestre – This is one of the weirdest novels I've read and is mysterious in the way vodou is. You'll never think about butterflies the same way.

Haitian Revolutionary Fictions: An Anthology, edited by Professor Marlene L. Daut Ph.D, Grégory Pierrot, Marion C. Rohrleitner – Another treasure trove. A recently released tome of fiction from and about Haiti. Invaluable in our attempt to preserve and continue making these stories.

Toussaint Louverture: A Revolutionary Life, by Phillipe Girard – My second favorite biography of Toussaint, outside of The Black Jacobins. Toussaint was a complex person, but who isn't?

About the Author

Dominick Rabrun is a writer, voice actor, and multimedia artist. He has narrated stories for *Escape Pod*, *Podcastle*, *Beneath Ceaseless Skies*, and other online publications. His work merges technology, storytelling, and music into a cohesive creative system. Guided by his first-generation Haitian-American heritage, conservative Christian upbringing, and 15 years of experience as a federal em-

ployee, Dominick has developed a philosophy called
"Vèvè-Punk," blending Haitian Vodou symbolism with
futuristic Afro-Caribbean themes. His practice ex-
plores the fragmented parts of his worldview and in-
vites audiences to investigate their own intersecting
identities. He lives in Hyattsville, Maryland. This is his
first book.

www.ingramcontent.com/pod-product-compliance
Lightning Source LLC
Chambersburg PA
CBHW022048050726
47591CB00002B/450